WELCOME to CAMP NIGHTMARE

WELCOME to CAMP NIGHTMARE

R.L. STINE

SCHOLASTIC INC.

NEW YORK TORONTO LONDON AUCKLAND
SYDNEY MEXICO CITY NEW DELHI HONG KONG

ISBN 978-0-545-15889-3

Goosebumps book series created by Parachute Press, Inc.
Copyright © 1993 by Scholastic Inc.

12 11 10 9 8 7   15/0

Printed in the U.S.A.   40
First printing, April 2010

"Behind the Screams" bonus material by Matthew D. Payne

I stared out the dusty window as the camp bus bounced over the narrow, winding road. I could see sloping red hills in the distance beneath a bright yellow sky.

Stumpy white trees lined the road like fence posts. We were way out in the wilderness. We hadn't passed a house or a farm for nearly an hour.

The bus seats were made of hard blue plastic. When the bus hit a bump, we all bounced up off our seats. Everyone laughed and shouted. The driver kept growling at us, yelling for us to pipe down.

There were twenty-two kids going to camp on the bus. I was sitting in the back row on the aisle, so I could count them all.

There were eighteen boys and only four girls. I guessed that the boys were all going to Camp Nightmoon, which is where I was going. The girls were going to a girls' camp nearby.

The girls sat together in the front rows and talked quietly to each other. Every once in a while, they'd glance back quickly to check out the boys.

The boys were a lot louder than the girls, cracking jokes, laughing, making funny noises, shouting out dumb things. It was a long bus ride, but we were having a good time.

The boy next to me was named Mike. He had the window seat. Mike looked a little like a bulldog. He was kind of chubby, with a round face and pudgy arms and legs. He had short, spiky black hair, which he scratched a lot. He was wearing baggy brown shorts and a sleeveless green T-shirt.

We had been sitting together the whole trip, but Mike didn't say much. I figured he was shy, or maybe very nervous. He told me this was his first time at sleepaway camp.

It was my first time, too. And I have to admit that, as the bus took me farther and farther from my home, I was already starting to miss my mom and dad just a little.

I'm twelve, but I've never really stayed away from home before. Even though the long bus ride was fun, I had this sad kind of feeling. And I think Mike was feeling the same way.

He pressed his chubby face against the window glass and stared out at the red hills rolling by in the distance.

"Are you okay, Mike?" I asked.

"Yeah. Sure, Billy," he replied quickly without turning around.

I thought about my mom and dad. Back at the bus station, they had seemed so serious. I guess they were nervous, too, about me going off to camp for the first time.

"We'll write every day," Dad said.

"Do your best," Mom said, hugging me harder than usual.

What a weird thing to say. Why didn't she say, "Have a good time"? Why did she say, "Do your best"?

As you can tell, I'm a bit of a worrier.

The only other boys I'd met so far were the two in the seat in front of us. One was named Colin. He had long brown hair down to his collar, and he wore silver sunglasses so you couldn't see his eyes. He acted kind of tough, and he wore a red bandanna on his forehead. He kept tying and untying the bandanna.

Sitting next to him in the seat on the aisle was a big, loud kid named Jay. Jay talked a lot about sports and kept bragging about what a good athlete he was. He liked showing off his big, muscular arms, especially when one of the girls turned around to check us out.

Jay teased Colin a lot and kept wrestling with him, gripping Colin's head in a headlock and messing up Colin's bandanna. You know. Just kidding around.

Jay had wild, bushy red hair that looked as if it had never been brushed. He had big blue eyes. He never stopped grinning and horsing around. He spent the whole trip telling gross jokes and shouting things at the girls.

"Hey — what's your name?" Jay called to a blond-haired girl who sat at the front by the window.

She ignored him for a long time. But the fourth time Jay called out the question, she turned around, her green eyes flashing. "Dawn," she replied. Then she pointed to the red-haired girl next to her. "And this is my friend Dori."

"Hey — that's amazing! My name is Dawn, too!" Jay joked.

A lot of the guys laughed, but Dawn didn't crack a smile. "Nice to meet you, Dawn," she called back to him. Then she turned around to the front.

The bus bounced over a hole in the road, and we all bounced with it.

"Hey, look, Billy," Mike said suddenly, pointing out the window.

Mike hadn't said anything for a long time. I leaned toward the window, trying to see what he was pointing at.

"I think I saw a prairie cat," he said, still staring hard.

"Huh? Really?" I saw a clump of low white trees and a lot of jagged red rocks. But I couldn't see any prairie cats.

4

"It went behind those rocks," Mike said, still pointing. Then he turned toward me. "Have you seen any towns or anything?"

I shook my head. "Just desert."

"But isn't the camp supposed to be near a town?" Mike looked worried.

"I don't think so," I told him. "My dad told me that Camp Nightmoon is past the desert, way out in the woods."

Mike thought about this for a while, frowning. "Well, what if we want to call home or something?" he asked.

"They probably have phones at the camp," I told him.

I glanced up in time to see Jay toss something up toward the girls at the front. It looked like a green ball. It hit Dawn on the back of the head and stuck in her blond hair.

"Hey!" Dawn cried out angrily. She pulled the sticky green ball from her hair. "What *is* this?" She turned to glare at Jay.

Jay giggled his high-pitched giggle. "I don't know. I found it stuck under the seat!" he called to her.

Dawn scowled at him and heaved the green ball back. It missed Jay and hit the rear window, where it stuck with a loud *plop*.

Everyone laughed. Dawn and her friend Dori made faces at Jay.

Colin fiddled with his red bandanna. Jay

5

slumped down low and raised his knees against the seat in front of him.

A few rows ahead of me, two grinning boys were singing a song we all knew but with really gross words replacing the original words.

A few other kids began to sing along.

Suddenly, without warning, the bus squealed to a stop, the tires skidding loudly over the road.

We all cried out in surprise. I bounced off my seat, and my chest hit the seat in front of me.

"Ugh!" That hurt.

As I slid back in the seat, my heart still pounding, the bus driver stood up and turned to us, leaning heavily into the aisle.

"Ohh!" Several loud gasps filled the bus as we saw the driver's face.

His head was enormous and pink, topped with a mop of wild bright blue hair that stood straight up. He had long, pointed ears. His huge red eyeballs bulged out from their dark sockets, bouncing in front of his snoutlike nose. Sharp white fangs drooped from his gaping mouth. A green liquid oozed over his heavy black lips.

As we goggled in silent horror, the driver tilted back his monstrous head and uttered an animal roar.

The driver roared so loud, the bus windows rattled.

Several kids shrieked in fright.

Mike and I both ducked down low, hiding behind the seat in front of us.

"He's turned into a *monster*!" Mike whispered, his eyes wide with fear.

Then we heard laughter at the front of the bus.

I raised myself up in time to see the bus driver reach one hand up to his bright blue hair. He tugged — and his face slid right off!

"Ohhh!" Several kids shrieked in horror.

But we quickly realized that the face dangling from the driver's hand was a mask. He had been wearing a rubber monster mask.

His real face was perfectly normal, I saw with relief. He had pale skin, short, thinning black hair, and tiny blue eyes. He laughed, shaking his head, enjoying his joke.

"This fools 'em every time!" he declared, holding up the ugly mask.

A few kids laughed along with him. But most of us were too surprised and confused to think it was funny.

Suddenly, his expression changed. "Everybody out!" he ordered gruffly.

He pulled a lever and the door slid open with a *whoosh*.

"Where are we?" someone called out.

But the driver ignored the question. He tossed the mask onto the driver's seat. Then, lowering his head so he wouldn't bump the roof, he quickly made his way out the door.

I leaned across Mike and stared out the window, but I couldn't see much. Just mile after mile of flat yellow ground, broken occasionally by clumps of red rock. It looked like a desert.

"Why are we getting out here?" Mike asked, turning to me. I could see he was really worried.

"Maybe this is the camp," I joked. Mike didn't think that was funny.

We were all confused as we pushed and shoved our way off the bus. Mike and I were the last ones off since we were sitting in the back.

As I stepped onto the hard ground, I shielded my eyes against the bright sunlight high in the afternoon sky. We were in a flat, open area. The bus was parked beside a concrete platform, about the size of a tennis court.

"It must be some kind of bus station or something," I told Mike. "You know. A drop-off point."

He had his hands shoved into the pockets of his shorts. He kicked at the dirt but didn't say anything.

On the other side of the platform, Jay was messing around with a boy I hadn't met yet. Colin was leaning against the side of the bus, being cool. The four girls were standing in a circle near the front of the platform, talking quietly about something.

I watched the driver walk over to the side of the bus and pull open the luggage compartment. He began pulling out bags and camp trunks and carrying them to the concrete platform.

A couple of guys had sat down on the edge of the platform to watch the driver work. Across the platform, Jay and the other guy started a contest, tossing little red pebbles as far as they could.

Mike, his hands still buried in his pockets, stepped up behind the sweating bus driver. "Hey, where are we? Why are we stopping here?" Mike asked him nervously.

The driver slid a heavy black trunk from the back of the luggage compartment. He completely ignored Mike's questions. Mike asked them again. And again the driver pretended Mike wasn't there.

Mike made his way back to where I was

standing, walking slowly, dragging his shoes across the hard ground. He looked really worried.

I was confused, but I wasn't worried. I mean, the bus driver was calmly going about his business, unloading the bus. He knew what he was doing.

"Why won't he answer me? Why won't he tell us anything?" Mike demanded.

I felt bad that Mike was so nervous. But I didn't want to hear any more of his questions. He was starting to make me nervous, too.

I wandered away from him, making my way along the side of the platform to where the four girls were standing. Across the platform, Jay and his buddies were still having their stone-throwing contest.

Dawn smiled at me as I came closer. Then she glanced quickly away. *She's really pretty*, I thought. Her blond hair gleamed in the bright sunlight.

"Are you from Center City?" her friend Dori asked, squinting at me, her freckled face twisted against the sun.

"No," I told her. "I'm from Midlands. It's north of Center City. Near Outreach Bay."

"I *know* where Midlands is!" Dori snapped snottily. The other three girls laughed.

I could feel myself blushing.

"What's your name?" Dawn asked, staring at me with her green eyes.

"Billy," I told her.

"My bird's name is Billy!" she exclaimed, and the girls all laughed again.

"Where are you girls going?" I asked quickly, eager to change the subject. "I mean, what camp?"

"Camp Nightmoon. There's one for boys and one for girls," Dori answered. "This is an all–Camp Nightmoon bus."

"Is your camp near ours?" I asked. I didn't even know there was a Camp Nightmoon for girls.

Dori shrugged. "We don't know," Dawn replied. "This is our first year."

"All of us," Dori added.

"Me, too," I told them. "I wonder why we stopped here."

The girls all shrugged.

I saw that Mike was lingering behind me, looking even more scared. I turned and made my way back to him.

"Look. The driver is finished carrying out our stuff," he said, pointing.

I turned in time to see the driver slam the luggage compartment door shut.

"What's happening?" Mike cried. "Is someone picking us up here? Why did he unload all our stuff?"

"I'll go find out," I said quietly. I started to jog over to the driver. He was standing in front of the open bus door, mopping his perspiring

11

forehead with the short sleeve of his tan driver's uniform.

He saw me coming — and quickly climbed into the bus. He slid into the driver's seat, pulling a green sun visor down over his forehead as I stepped up to the door.

"Is someone coming for us?" I called in to him.

To my surprise, he pulled the lever, and the bus door slammed shut in my face.

The engine started up with a roar and a burst of gray exhaust fumes.

"Hey!" I screamed, and pounded angrily on the glass door.

I had to leap back as the bus squealed away, its tires spinning noisily on the hard dirt. "Hey!" I shouted. "You don't have to run me over!"

I stared angrily as the bus bounced onto the road and roared away. Then I turned back to Mike. He was standing beside the four girls. They were all looking upset now.

"He — he left," Mike stammered as I approached them. "He just *left* us here in the middle of nowhere."

We gazed down the road at the bus until it disappeared over the darkening horizon. We all grew very quiet.

A few seconds later, we heard the frightening animal cries.

Very close. And getting closer.

3

"Wh-what's that?" Mike stammered.

We turned in the direction of the shrill cries.

They seemed to be coming from across the platform. At first, I thought that Jay and Colin and their friends were playing a joke on us, making the animal cries to frighten us.

But then I saw the scared, wide-eyed expressions on their faces. Jay, Colin, and the others had frozen in place. They weren't making the noises.

The cries grew louder. Closer.

Shrill warnings.

And then, staring into the distance beyond the platform, I saw them. Small, dark creatures, keeping low, rolling rapidly along the flat ground, tossing their heads back and uttering excited shrieks as they came toward us.

"What are they?" Mike cried, moving close to me.

"Are they prairie wolves?" Dori asked in a trembling voice.

"I hope not!" one of the other girls called out.

We all climbed onto the concrete platform and huddled behind our trunks and bags.

The animal cries grew louder as the creatures drew near. I could see dozens of them. They scurried toward us over the flat ground as if being blown by the wind.

"Help! Somebody *help* us!" I heard Mike scream.

Next to me, Jay still had two of the red pebbles from his stone-throwing competition in his hand. "Pick up rocks!" he was shouting frantically. "Maybe we can scare them away!"

The creatures stopped a few yards from the concrete platform and raised themselves up menacingly on their hind feet.

Huddled between Mike and Jay, I could see them clearly now. They were wolves or wildcats of some sort. Standing upright, they were nearly three feet tall.

They had slender, almost scrawny bodies covered with spotty red-brown fur. Their paws had long silvery claws growing out of them. Their heads were nearly as slender as their bodies. Tiny red weasel eyes stared hungrily at us. Their long mouths snapped open and shut, revealing double rows of silvery, daggerlike teeth.

"No! No! Help!" Mike dropped to his knees. His entire body convulsed in a shudder of terror.

14

Some of the kids were crying. Others gaped at the advancing creatures in stunned silence.

I was too scared to cry out or move or do *anything*.

I stared at the row of creatures, my heart thudding, my mouth as dry as cotton.

The creatures grew silent. Standing a few feet from the platform, they eyed us, snapping their jaws loudly, hungrily. White froth began to drip from their mouths.

"They — they're going to attack!" a boy yelled.

"They look hungry!" I heard one of the girls say.

The white froth poured thickly over their pointed teeth. They continued to snap their jaws. It sounded like a dozen steel traps being snapped shut.

Suddenly, one of them leaped onto the edge of the platform.

"No!" several kids cried out in unison.

We huddled closer together, trying to stay behind the pile of trunks and bags.

Another creature climbed onto the platform. Then three more.

I took a step back.

I saw Jay pull back his arm and heave a red rock at one of the frothing creatures. The rock hit the platform with a *crack* and bounced away.

The creatures were not frightened. They arched their backs, preparing to attack.

They began to make a high-pitched chattering sound.

And moved nearer. Nearer.

Jay threw another rock.

This one hit one of the advancing creatures on the side. It uttered a shrill *eek* of surprise. But it kept moving steadily forward, its red eyes trained on Jay, its jaws snapping hungrily.

"Go away!" Dori cried in a trembling voice. "Go home! Go away! Go *away*!"

But her shouts had no effect.

The creatures advanced.

"Run!" I urged. "Run!"

"We can't outrun them!" someone shouted.

The shrill chittering grew louder. Deafening. Until it seemed as if we were surrounded by a wall of sound.

The ugly creatures lowered themselves to pounce.

"Run!" I repeated. "Come on — run!"

My legs wouldn't cooperate. They felt rubbery and weak.

Trying to back away from the attacking creatures, I toppled over backward off the platform.

I saw flashing stars as the back of my head hit the hard ground.

They're going to get me, I realized.

I can't get away.

I heard the sirenlike attack cry.

I heard the scrape of the creatures' long claws over the concrete platform.

I heard the screams and cries of the frightened campers.

Then, as I struggled frantically to pull myself up, I heard the deafening roar.

At first I thought it was an explosion.

I thought the platform had blown up.

But then I turned and saw the rifle.

Another explosion of gunfire. White smoke filled the air.

The creatures spun around and darted away, silent now, their scraggly fur scraping the ground as they kept low, their tails between their furry legs.

"Ha-ha! Look at 'em run!" A man kept a rifle poised on his shoulder as he watched the creatures retreat.

Behind him stood a long green bus.

I pulled myself up and brushed myself off.

Everyone was laughing now, jumping up and down joyfully, celebrating the narrow escape.

I was still too shaken up to celebrate.

"They're running like jackrabbits!" the man declared in a booming voice. He lowered the rifle.

It took me a while to realize he had come out of the camp bus to rescue us. We hadn't heard or seen the bus pull up because of the attack cries of the animals.

"Are you okay, Mike?" I asked, walking over to my frightened-looking new friend.

"I guess," he replied uncertainly. "I guess I'm okay now."

Dawn slapped me on the back, grinning. "We're okay!" she cried. "We're all okay!"

We gathered in front of the man with the rifle.

He was big and red-faced, mostly bald except for a fringe of curly yellow hair around his head. He had a blond mustache under an enormous beak of a nose and tiny black bird eyes beneath bushy blond eyebrows.

"Hi, guys! I'm Uncle Al. I'm your friendly camp director. I hope you enjoyed that welcome to Camp Nightmoon!" he boomed in a deep voice.

I heard muttered replies.

He leaned the rifle against the bus and took a few steps toward us, studying our faces. He was wearing white shorts and a bright green camp

18

T-shirt that stretched over his big belly. Two young guys, also in green and white, stepped out of the bus, serious expressions on their faces.

"Let's load up," Uncle Al instructed them in his deep voice.

He didn't apologize for being late.

He didn't explain about the weird animals. And he didn't ask if we were okay after that scare.

The two counselors began dragging the camp trunks and shoving them into the luggage compartment on the bus.

"Looks like a good group this year," Uncle Al shouted. "We'll drop you girls off first across the river. Then we'll get you boys settled in."

"What *were* those awful animals?" Dori called to Uncle Al.

He didn't seem to hear her.

We began climbing onto the bus. I looked for Mike and found him near the end of the line. His face was pale, and he still looked really shaken. "I — I was really scared," he admitted.

"But we're okay," I reassured him. "Now we can relax and have fun."

"I'm so hungry," Mike complained. "I haven't eaten all day."

One of the counselors overheard him. "You won't be hungry when you taste the camp food," he told Mike.

We piled into the bus. I sat next to Mike. I could hear the poor guy's stomach growling. I suddenly realized I was starving, too. And I was really eager to see what Camp Nightmoon looked like. I hoped it wouldn't be a long bus ride to get there.

"How far away is our camp?" I called to Uncle Al, who had slid into the driver's seat.

He didn't seem to hear me.

"Hey, Mike, we're on our way!" I said happily as the bus pulled onto the road.

Mike forced a smile. "I'm so glad to get *away* from there!"

To my surprise, the bus ride took less than five minutes.

We all muttered our shock at what a short trip it was. Why hadn't the first bus taken us all the way?

A big wooden sign proclaiming CAMP NIGHTMOON came into view, and Uncle Al turned the bus onto a gravel road that led through a patch of short trees into the camp.

We followed the narrow, winding road across a green river. Several small cabins came into view. "Girls' camp," Uncle Al announced. The bus stopped to let the four girls off. Dawn waved to me as she climbed down.

A few minutes later, we pulled into the boys' camp. Through the bus window I could see a row of small white cabins. On top of a gently sloping hill stood a large white-shingled building, probably a meeting lodge or mess hall.

At the edge of a field, three counselors, all dressed in white shorts and green T-shirts, were working to start a fire in a large stone barbecue pit.

"Hey, we're going to have a cookout!" I exclaimed to Mike. I was starting to feel really excited.

Mike smiled, too. He was practically drooling at the thought of food!

The bus came to an abrupt stop at the end of the row of small bunks. Uncle Al pulled himself up quickly from the driver's seat and turned to us. "Welcome to beautiful Camp Nightmoon!" he bellowed. "Step down and line up for your bunk assignments. Once you get unpacked and have dinner, I'll see you at the campfire."

We pushed our way noisily out of the bus. I saw Jay enthusiastically slapping another boy on the back. I think we were all feeling a lot better, forgetting about our close call.

I stepped down and took a deep breath. The cool air smelled really sweet and fresh. I saw a long row of short evergreen trees behind the white lodge on the hill.

As I took my place in line, I searched for the waterfront. I could hear the soft rush of the river behind a thick row of evergreens, but I couldn't see it.

Mike, Jay, Colin, and I were assigned to the same bunk. It was Bunk 4. I thought the bunk

21

should have a more interesting name. But it just had a number. Bunk 4.

It was really small, with a low ceiling and windows on two sides. It was just big enough for six campers. There were bunk beds against three walls and a tall dresser on the fourth wall, with a little square of space in the middle.

There was no bathroom. I guessed it was in another building.

As the four of us entered the bunk, we saw that one of the beds had already been claimed. It had been carefully made, the green blanket tucked in neatly, some sports magazines and a radio resting on top.

"That must belong to our counselor," Jay said, inspecting the radio.

"Hope we don't have to wear those ugly green T-shirts," Colin said, grinning. He was still wearing his silver sunglasses, even though the sun was nearly down and it was just about as dark as night in the cabin.

Jay claimed a top bunk, and Colin took the bed beneath his.

"Can I have a lower one?" Mike asked me. "I roll around a lot at night. I'm afraid I might fall out of a top one."

"Yeah. Sure. No problem," I replied. I wanted the top bunk anyway. It would be a lot more fun.

"Hope you guys don't snore," Colin said.

"We're not going to sleep in here anyway," Jay said. "We're going to party all night!" He playfully slapped Mike on the back, so hard that Mike went sprawling into the dresser.

"Hey!" Mike whined. "That hurt!"

"Sorry. Guess I don't know my own strength," Jay replied, grinning at Colin.

The cabin door opened, and a redheaded guy with dark freckles all over his face walked in, carrying a big gray plastic bag. He was tall and very skinny and was wearing white shorts and a green camp T-shirt.

"Hey, guys," he said, and dropped the large bag on the cabin floor with a groan. He checked us out, then pointed to the bag. "There's your bed stuff," he said. "Make your beds. Try to make them as neat as mine." He pointed to the bunk against the window with the radio on it.

"Are you our counselor?" I asked.

He nodded. "Yeah. I'm the lucky one." He turned and started to walk out.

"What's your name?" Jay called after him.

"Larry," he said, pushing open the cabin door. "Your trunks will be here in a few minutes," he told us. "You can fight it out over drawer space. Two of the drawers are stuck shut."

He started out the door, then turned back to us. "Keep away from my stuff." The door slammed hard behind him.

Peering out the window, I watched him lope away, taking long, fast strides, bobbing his head as he walked.

"Great guy," Colin muttered sarcastically.

"Real friendly," Jay added, shaking his head.

Then we dived into the plastic bag and pulled out sheets and wool blankets. Jay and Colin got into a wrestling match over a blanket they claimed was softer than the others.

I tossed a sheet onto my mattress and started to climb up to tuck it in.

I was halfway up the ladder when I heard Mike scream.

Mike was right beneath me, making his bed. He screamed so loud, I cried out and nearly fell off the ladder.

I leaped off the ladder, my heart pounding, and stepped beside him.

Staring straight ahead, his mouth wide open in horror, Mike backed away from his bed.

"Mike — what's wrong?" I asked. "What *is* it?"

"S-snakes!" Mike stammered, staring straight ahead at his unmade bed as he backed away.

"Huh?" I followed his gaze. It was too dark to see anything.

Colin laughed. "Not *that* old joke!" he cried.

"Larry put rubber snakes in your bed," Jay said, grinning as he stepped up beside us.

"They're not rubber! They're real!" Mike insisted, his voice trembling.

Jay laughed and shook his head. "I can't believe

you fell for that old gag." He took a few steps toward the bed — then stopped. "Hey!"

I moved close, and the two snakes came into focus. Raising themselves from the shadows, they arched their heads, pulling back as if preparing to attack.

"They're real!" Jay cried, turning back to Colin. "Two of them!"

"Probably not poisonous," Colin said, venturing closer.

The two let out angry hisses, raising themselves high off the bed. They were very long and skinny. Their heads were wider than their bodies. Their tongues flicked from side to side as they arched themselves menacingly.

"I'm scared of snakes," Mike uttered in a soft voice.

"They're probably scared of *you!*" Jay joked, slapping Mike on the back.

Mike winced. He was in no mood for Jay's horseplay. "We've got to get Larry or somebody," Mike said.

"No way!" Jay insisted. "You can handle 'em, Mike. There's only two of them!"

Jay gave Mike a playful shove toward the bed. He only meant to give him a scare.

But Mike stumbled — and fell onto the bed.

The snakes darted in unison.

I saw one of them clamp its teeth into Mike's hand.

Mike raised himself to his feet. He didn't react at first. Then he uttered a high-pitched shriek.

Two drops of blood appeared on the back of his right hand. He stared down at them, then grabbed the hand.

"It *bit* me!" he shrieked.

"Oh, no!" I cried.

"Did it puncture the skin?" Colin asked. "Is it bleeding?"

Jay rushed forward and grabbed Mike's shoulder. "Hey, man — I'm really sorry," he said. "I didn't mean to —"

Mike groaned in pain. "It — really hurts," he whispered. He was breathing really hard, his chest heaving, making weird noises as he breathed.

The snakes, coiled in the middle of his lower bunk, began to hiss again.

"You'd better hurry to the nurse," Jay said, his hand still on Mike's shoulder. "I'll come with you."

"N-no," Mike stammered. His face was as pale as a ghost's. He held his hand tightly. "I'll go find her!" He burst out of the cabin, running at full speed. The door slammed behind him.

"Hey — I didn't mean to push him, you know," Jay explained to us. I could see he was really upset. "I was just joking, just trying to scare him a little. I didn't mean for him to fall or anything. . . ." His voice trailed off.

27

"What are we going to do about *them*?" I asked, pointing at the two coiled snakes.

"I'll get Larry," Colin offered. He started toward the door.

"No, wait." I called him back. "Look. They've moved onto Mike's sheet, right?"

Jay and Colin followed my gaze to the bed. The snakes arched themselves high, preparing to bite again.

"So?" Jay asked, scratching his disheveled hair.

"So we can wrap them up in the sheet and carry them outside," I said.

Jay stared at me. "Wish I'd thought of that. Let's do it, man!"

"You'll get bit," Colin warned.

I stared at the snakes. They seemed to be studying me, too. "They can't bite us through the sheet," I said.

"They can try!" Colin exclaimed, hanging back.

"If we're fast enough," I said, taking a cautious step toward the bed, "we can wrap them up before they know what's happening."

The snakes hissed out a warning, drawing themselves higher.

"How did they get in here, anyway?" Colin asked.

"Maybe the camp is *crawling* with snakes," Jay

said, grinning. "Maybe you've got some in *your* bed, too, Colin!" He laughed.

"Let's get serious here," I said sternly, my eyes locked on the coiled snakes. "Are we going to try this or not?"

"Yeah. Let's do it," Jay answered. "I mean, I owe it to Mike."

Colin remained silent.

"I'll bet I could grab one by the tail and swing him out through the window," Jay said. "You could grab the tail end of the other one and —"

"Let's try my plan first," I suggested quietly.

We crept over to the snakes, sneaking up on them. It was kind of silly since they were staring right at us.

I pointed to one end of the sheet, which was folded up onto the bed. "Grab it there," I instructed Jay. "Then pull it up."

He hesitated. "What if I miss? Or you miss?"

"Then we're in trouble," I replied grimly. My eyes on the snakes, I reached my hand forward to the other corner of the sheet. "Ready? On three," I whispered.

My heart was in my mouth. I could barely choke out, "One, two, three."

At the count of three, we both grabbed for the ends of the sheet.

"Pull!" I cried in a shrill voice I couldn't believe was coming from me.

We pulled up the sheet and brought the ends together, making a bundle.

At the bottom of the bundle, the snakes wriggled frantically. I heard their jaws snap. They wriggled so hard, the bottom of the bundle swung back and forth.

"They don't like this," Jay said as we hurried to the door, carrying our wriggling, swaying bundle between us, trying to keep our bodies as far away from it as possible.

I pushed open the door with my shoulder, and we ran out onto the grass.

"Now what?" Jay asked.

"Keep going," I replied. I could see one of the snakes poking its head out. "Hurry!"

We ran past the cabins toward a small clump of shrubs. Beyond the shrubs stood a patch of low trees. When we reached the trees, we swung the bundle back, then heaved the whole sheet into the trees.

It opened as it fell to the ground. The two snakes slithered out instantly and pulled themselves to shelter under the trees.

Jay and I let out loud sighs of relief. We stood there for a moment, hunched over, hands on our knees, trying to catch our breath.

Crouching down, I looked for the snakes. But they had slithered deep into the safety of the evergreens.

I stood up. "I guess we should take back Mike's sheet," I said.

"He probably won't want to sleep on it," Jay said. But he reached down and pulled it up from the grass. He balled it up and tossed it to me. "It's probably dripping with snake venom," he said, making a disgusted face.

When we got back to the cabin, Colin had made his bed and was busily unpacking the contents of his trunk, shoving everything into the top dresser drawer. He turned as we entered. "How'd it go?" he asked casually.

"Horrible," Jay replied quickly, his expression grim. "We both got bit. Twice."

"You're a terrible liar!" Colin told him, laughing. "You shouldn't even try."

Jay laughed, too.

Colin turned to me. "You're a hero," he said.

"Thanks for all your help," Jay told him sarcastically.

Colin started to reply. But the cabin door opened, and Larry poked his freckled face in. "How's it going?" he asked. "You're not finished yet?"

"We had a little problem," Jay told him.

"Where's the fourth guy? The chubby one?" Larry asked, lowering his head so he wouldn't bump it on the door frame as he stepped inside.

"Mike got bit. By a snake," I told him.

"There were two snakes in his bed," Jay added.

Larry's expression didn't change. He didn't seem at all surprised. "So where did Mike go?" he asked casually, swatting a mosquito on his arm.

"His hand was bleeding. He went to the nurse to get it taken care of," I told him.

"Huh?" Larry's mouth dropped open.

"He went to find the nurse," I repeated.

Larry tossed back his head and started to laugh. "Nurse?" he cried, laughing hard. "*What* nurse?!"

The door opened and Mike returned, still holding his wounded hand. His face was pale, his expression frightened. "They said there was no nurse," he told me.

Then he saw Larry sitting on his bunk. "Larry — my hand," Mike said. He held the hand out so the counselor could see it. It was stained with bright red blood.

Larry stood up. "I think I have some bandages," he told Mike. He pulled out a slender black case from beneath his bunk and began to search through it.

Mike stood beside him, holding up his hand. Drops of blood splashed on the cabin floor. "They said the camp doesn't have a nurse," Mike repeated.

Larry shook his head. "If you get hurt in *this* camp," he told Mike seriously, "you're on your own."

"I think my hand is swelling a little," Mike said.

Larry handed him a roll of bandages. "The washroom is at the end of this row of cabins," he told Mike, closing the case and shoving it back under the bed. "Go wash the hand and bandage it. Hurry. It's almost dinnertime."

Holding the bandages tightly in his good hand, Mike hurried off to follow Larry's instructions.

"By the way, how'd you guys get the snakes out of here?" Larry asked, glancing around the cabin.

"We carried them out in Mike's sheet," Jay told him. He pointed at me. "It was Billy's idea."

Larry stared hard at me. "Hey, I'm impressed, Billy," he said. "That was pretty brave, man."

"Maybe I inherited something from my parents," I told him. "They're scientists. Explorers, kind of. They go off for months at a time, exploring the wildest places."

"Well, Camp Nightmoon is pretty wild," Larry said. "And you guys had better be careful. I'm warning you." His expression turned serious. "There's no nurse at Camp Nightmoon. Uncle Al doesn't believe in coddling you guys."

The hot dogs were all charred black, but we were so hungry, we didn't care. I shoved three of them down in less than five minutes. I don't think I'd ever been so hungry in all my life.

The campfire was in a flat clearing surrounded by a circle of round white stones. Behind us, the large white-shingled lodge loomed over the sloping hill. Ahead of us a thick line of evergreen trees formed a fence that hid the river from view.

Through a small gap in the trees, I could see a flickering campfire in the distance on the other side of the river. I wondered if that was the campfire of the girls' camp.

I thought about Dawn and Dori. I wondered if the two camps ever got together, if I'd ever see them again.

Dinner around the big campfire seemed to put everyone in a good mood. Jay was the only one sitting near me who complained about the hot dogs being burned. But I think he put away four or five of them anyway!

Mike had trouble eating because of his bandaged hand. When he dropped his first hot dog, I thought he was going to burst into tears. By the end of dinner, he was in a much better mood. His wounded hand had swelled up just a little. But he said it didn't hurt as much as before.

The counselors were easy to spot. They all wore their identical white shorts and green T-shirts. There were eight or ten of them, all young guys probably sixteen or seventeen. They ate together quietly, away from us campers. I kept looking at Larry, but he never once turned around to look at any of us.

I was thinking about Larry, trying to figure out if he was shy or if he just didn't like us campers very much. Suddenly, Uncle Al climbed to his feet and motioned with both hands for us all to be quiet.

"I want to welcome you boys to Camp Nightmoon," he began. "I hope you're all unpacked and comfortable in your bunks. I know that most of you are first-time campers."

He was speaking quickly, without any pauses between sentences, as if he was running through this for the thousandth time and wanted to get it over with.

"I'd like to tell you some of our basic rules," he continued. "First, lights-out is at nine sharp."

A lot of guys groaned.

"You might think you can ignore this rule," Uncle Al continued, paying no attention to their reaction. "You might think you can sneak out of your cabins to meet or take a walk by the river. But I'm warning you now that we don't allow it, and we have very good ways of making sure this rule is obeyed."

He paused to clear his throat.

Some boys were giggling about something. Across from me, Jay burped loudly, which caused more giggles.

Uncle Al didn't seem to hear any of this. "On the other side of the river is the girls' camp," he continued loudly, motioning to the trees. "You might be able to see their campfire. Well, I want to make it clear that swimming or rowing over to the girls' camp is strictly forbidden."

Several boys groaned loudly. This made everyone laugh. Even some of the counselors laughed. Uncle Al remained grim-faced.

"The woods around Camp Nightmoon are filled with grizzlies and tree bears," Uncle Al continued. "They come to the river to bathe and to drink. And they're usually hungry."

This caused another big reaction from all of us sitting around the fading campfire. Someone made a loud growling sound. Another kid screamed. Then everyone laughed.

"You won't be laughing if a bear claws your head off," Uncle Al said sternly.

He turned to the group of counselors outside our circle. "Larry, Kurt, come over here," he ordered.

The two counselors climbed obediently to their feet and made their way to the center of the circle beside Uncle Al.

"I want you two to demonstrate to the new campers the procedure to follow when — er, I mean, *if* — you are attacked by a grizzly bear."

Immediately, the two counselors dropped to the ground on their stomachs. They lay flat and covered the backs of their heads with their hands.

"That's right. I hope you're all paying close attention," the camp director thundered at us.

"Cover your neck and head. Try your best not to move." He motioned to the two counselors. "Thanks, guys. You can get up."

"Have there ever been any bear attacks here?" I called out, cupping my hands so Uncle Al could hear me.

He turned in my direction. "Two last summer," he replied.

Several boys gasped.

"It wasn't pretty," Uncle Al continued. "It's hard to remain still when a huge bear is pawing you and drooling all over you. But if you move . . ." His voice trailed off, leaving the rest to our imaginations, I guess.

I felt a cold shiver run down my back. I didn't want to think about bears and bear attacks.

What kind of camp did Mom and Dad send me to? I found myself wondering. I couldn't wait to call them and tell them about all that had happened already.

Uncle Al waited for everyone to quiet down, then pointed off to the side. "Do you see that cabin over there?" he asked.

In the dim evening light, I could make out a cabin standing halfway up the hill toward the lodge. It appeared to be a little larger than the other cabins. It seemed to be built on a slant, sort of tipping on its side, as if the wind had tried to blow it over.

"I want you to make sure you see that cabin,"

Uncle Al warned, his voice thundering out above the crackling of the purple fire. "That is known as the Forbidden Bunk. We don't talk about that bunk — and we don't go near it."

I felt another cold shiver as I stared through the gray evening light at the shadowy, tilted cabin. I felt a sharp sting on the back of my neck and slapped a mosquito, too late to keep it from biting me.

"I'm going to repeat what I just said," Uncle Al shouted, still pointing to the dark cabin on the hill. "That is known as the Forbidden Bunk. It has been closed and boarded up for many years. No one is to go near that cabin. *No one.*"

This started everyone talking and laughing. Nervous laughter, I think.

"Why is the Forbidden Bunk forbidden?" someone called out.

"We never talk about it," Uncle Al replied sharply.

Jay leaned over and whispered in my ear, "Let's go check it out."

I laughed. Then I turned back to Jay uncertainly. "You're kidding — right?"

He grinned in reply and didn't say anything.

I turned back toward the fire. Uncle Al was wishing us all a good stay and saying how much he was looking forward to camp this year. "And one more rule," he called out. "You must write to your parents every day. Every day! We want them to know what a great time you're having at Camp Nightmoon."

I saw Mike holding his wounded hand gingerly. "It's starting to throb," he told me, sounding very frightened.

"Maybe Larry has something to put on it," I said. "Let's go ask him."

Uncle Al dismissed us. We all climbed to our feet, stretching and yawning, and started to make our way in small groups back to the bunks.

Mike and I lingered behind, hoping to talk to Larry. We saw him talking to the other counselors. He was at least a head taller than all of them.

"Hey, Larry!" Mike called.

But by the time we pushed our way through the groups of kids heading the other way, Larry had disappeared.

"Maybe he's going to our bunk to make sure we obey lights-out," I suggested.

"Let's go see," Mike replied anxiously.

We walked quickly past the dying campfire. It had stopped crackling but still glowed a deep purple-red. Then we headed along the curve of the hill toward Bunk 4.

"My hand really hurts," Mike groaned, holding it tenderly in front of him. "I'm not just complaining. It's throbbing and it's swelling up. And I'm starting to have chills."

"Larry will know what to do," I replied, trying to sound reassuring.

"I hope so," Mike said shakily.

We both stopped when we heard the howls.

Hideous howls. Like an animal in pain. But too human to be from an animal.

Long, shrill howls that cut through the air and echoed down the hill.

Mike uttered a quiet gasp. He turned to me. Even in the darkness, I could see the fright on his face.

"Those cries," he whispered. "They're coming from . . . the Forbidden Bunk!"

7

A few minutes later, Mike and I trudged into the cabin. Jay and Colin were sitting tensely on their beds. "Where's Larry?" Mike asked, fear creeping into his voice.

"Not here," Colin replied.

"Where *is* he?" Mike demanded shrilly. "I've got to find him. My *hand*!"

"He should be here soon," Jay offered.

I could still hear the strange howls through the open window. "Do you hear that?" I asked, walking over to the window and listening hard.

"Probably a prairie cat," Colin said.

"Prairie cats don't howl," Mike told him. "Prairie cats screech, but they don't howl."

"How do you know?" Colin asked, walking over to Larry's bunk and sitting down on the bottom bed.

"We studied them in school," Mike replied.

Another howl made us all stop and listen.

"It sounds like a man," Jay offered, his eyes

lighting up excitedly. "A man who's been locked up in the Forbidden Bunk for years and years."

Mike swallowed hard. "Do you really think so?"

Jay and Colin laughed.

"What should I do about my hand?" Mike asked, holding it up. It was definitely swollen.

"Go wash it again," I told him. "And put a fresh bandage on it." I peered out the window into the darkness. "Maybe Larry will show up soon. He probably knows where to get something to put on it."

"I can't believe there's no nurse," Mike whined. "Why would my parents send me to a camp where there's no nurse or infirmary or anything?"

"Uncle Al doesn't like to coddle us," Colin said, repeating Larry's words.

Jay stood up and broke into an imitation of Uncle Al. "Stay away from the Forbidden Bunk!" he cried in a booming deep voice. He sounded a lot like him. "We don't talk about it and we don't ever go near it!"

We all laughed at Jay's impression. Even Mike.

"We should go there tonight!" Colin said enthusiastically. "We should check it out immediately!"

We heard another long, sorrowful howl roll down the hill from the direction of the Forbidden Bunk.

"I — I don't think we should," Mike said softly, examining his hand. He started for the door.

"I'm going to go wash this." The door slammed behind him.

"He's scared," Jay scoffed.

"I'm a little scared, too," I admitted. "I mean, those awful howls . . ."

Jay and Colin both laughed. "Every camp has something like the Forbidden Bunk. The camp director makes it up," Colin said.

"Yeah," Jay agreed. "Camp directors love scaring kids. It's the only fun they have."

He puffed out his chest and imitated Uncle Al again: "Don't leave the bunk after lights-out or you'll never be seen again!" he thundered, then burst out laughing.

"There's nothing in that Forbidden Bunk," Colin said, shaking his head. "It's probably completely empty. It's all just a joke. You know. Like camp ghost stories. Every camp has its own ghost story."

"How do you know?" I asked, dropping down onto Mike's bed. "Have you ever been to camp before?"

"No," Colin replied. "But I have friends who told me about *their* camp." He reached up and pulled off his silver sunglasses for the first time. He had bright sky-blue eyes, like big blue marbles.

We suddenly heard a bugle repeating a slow, sad-sounding tune.

"That must be the signal for lights-out," I said, yawning. I started to pull off my shoes. I was too

44

tired to change or wash up. I planned to sleep in my clothes.

"Let's sneak out and explore the Forbidden Bunk," Jay urged. "Come on. We can be the first ones to do it!"

I yawned again. "I'm really too tired," I told them.

"Me, too," Colin said. He turned to Jay. "How about tomorrow night?"

Jay's face fell in disappointment.

"Tomorrow," Colin insisted, kicking his shoes into the corner and starting to pull off his socks.

"I wouldn't do it if I were you!"

The voice startled all three of us. We turned to the window where Larry's head suddenly appeared from out of the darkness. He grinned in at us. "I'd listen to Uncle Al if I were you," he said.

How long had he been out there listening to us? I wondered. Was he deliberately *spying* on us?

The door opened. Larry lowered his head as he loped in. His grin had faded. "Uncle Al wasn't kidding around," he said seriously.

"Yeah. Sure," Colin replied sarcastically. He went over to his bed and slid beneath the wool blanket.

"I guess the camp ghost will get us if we go out after lights-out," Jay joked, tossing a towel across the room.

"No. No ghost," Larry said softly. "But Sabre

45

will." He pulled out his drawer and began searching for something inside it.

"Huh? Who's Sabre?" I asked, suddenly wide-awake.

"Sabre is an *it*," Larry answered mysteriously.

"Sabre is a red-eyed monster who eats a camper every night," Colin sneered. He stared at me. "There *is* no Sabre. Larry's just giving us another phony camp story."

Larry stopped searching his drawer and gazed up at Colin. "No, I'm not," he insisted in a low voice. "I'm trying to save you guys some trouble. I'm not trying to scare you."

"Then what is Sabre?" I asked impatiently.

Larry pulled a sweater from the drawer, then pushed the drawer shut. "You don't want to find out," he replied.

"Come on. Tell us what it is," I begged.

"He isn't going to," Colin said.

"I'll tell you guys only one thing. Sabre will rip your heart out," Larry said flatly.

Jay snickered. "Yeah. Sure."

"I'm serious!" Larry snapped. "I'm not kidding, you guys!" He pulled the sweater over his head. "You don't believe me? Go out one night. Go out and meet Sabre." He struggled to get his arm into the sweater sleeve. "But before you do," he warned, "leave me a note with your address so I'll know where to send your stuff."

We had fun the next morning.

We all woke up really early. The sun was just rising over the horizon to the south, and the air was still cool and damp. I could hear birds chirping.

The sound reminded me of home. As I lowered myself to the floor and stretched, I thought of my mom and dad and wished I could call them and tell them about the camp. But it was only the second day. I'd be too embarrassed to call them on the second day.

I was definitely homesick. But luckily there wasn't any time to feel sad. After we pulled on fresh clothes, we hurried up to the lodge on the hill, which served as a meeting hall, theater, and mess hall.

Long tables and benches were set up in straight rows in the center of the enormous room. The floorboards and walls were all dark redwood. Redwood ceiling beams crisscrossed high above our heads. There were very few windows, so it felt as if we were in an enormous dark cave.

The clatter of dishes and cups and silverware was deafening. Our shouts and laughter rang off the high ceiling, echoed off the hardwood walls. Mike shouted something to me from across the table, but I couldn't hear him because of the racket.

Some guys complained about the food, but I thought it was okay. We had scrambled egg squares, bacon strips, fried potatoes, and toast, with tall cups of juice. I never eat a breakfast that big at home. But I found that I was really starved, and I gobbled it up.

After breakfast we lined up outside the lodge to form different activity groups. The sun had climbed high in the sky. It was going to be really hot. Our excited voices echoed off the sloping hill. We were all laughing and talking, feeling good.

Larry and two other counselors, clipboards in hand, stood in front of us, shielding their eyes from the bright sun as they divided us into groups. The first group of about ten boys headed off to the river for a morning swim.

Some people have all the luck, I thought. I was eager to get to the waterfront and see what the river was like.

As I waited for my name to be called, I spotted a pay phone on the wall of the lodge. My parents flashed into my mind again. *Maybe I will call them later,* I decided. I was so eager to describe the camp to them and tell them about my new friends.

"Okay, guys. Follow me to the ball field," Larry instructed us. "We're going to play our first game of scratchball."

About twelve of us, including everyone from my bunk, followed Larry down the hill toward the flat grassy area that formed the playing field.

I jogged to catch up to Larry, who always seemed to walk at top speed, stretching out his long legs as if he were in a terrible hurry. "Are we going to swim after this?" I asked.

Without slowing his pace, he glanced at his clipboard. "Yeah. I guess," he replied. "You guys'll need a swim. We're going to work up a sweat."

"You ever play scratchball before?" Jay asked me as we hurried to keep up with Larry.

"Yeah. Sure," I replied. "We play it a lot in school."

Scratchball is an easy game to learn. The batter throws the ball in the air as high and as far as he can. Then he has to run the bases before someone on the other team catches the ball, tags him with it, or throws him out.

Larry stopped at the far corner of the wide green field, where the bases and batter's square had already been set up. He made us line up and divided us into two teams.

49

He started calling out names. But when he called out Mike's name, Mike stepped up to Larry, holding his bandaged hand tenderly. "I — I don't think I can play, Larry," Mike stammered.

"Come on, Mike. Don't whine," Larry snapped.

"But it really hurts," Mike insisted. "It's throbbing like crazy, Larry. The pain is shooting all the way up and down my side. And look" — he raised the hand to Larry's face — "it's all swelled up!"

Larry pushed the arm away gently with his clipboard. "Go sit in the shade," he told Mike.

"Shouldn't I get some medicine or something to put on it?" Mike asked shrilly. I could see the poor guy was really in bad shape.

"Just sit over there," Larry ordered, pointing to a clump of short leafy trees at the edge of the field. "We'll talk about it later."

Larry turned away from Mike and blew a whistle to start the game. "I'll take Mike's place on the Blue team," he announced, jogging onto the field.

I forgot about Mike as soon as the game got underway. We were having a lot of fun. Most of the guys were pretty good scratchball players, and we played much faster than my friends do back home at the playground.

My first time up at the batter's square, I heaved the ball really high. But it dropped right into a fielder's hands, and I was out. My second time up, I made it to three bases before I was tagged out.

Larry was a great player. When he came up to the batter's square, he tossed the ball harder than I ever saw anyone toss it. It sailed over the fielders' heads and, as they chased after it, Larry rounded all the bases, his long legs stretching out gracefully as he ran.

By the fourth inning, our team, the Blue team, was ahead twelve to six. We had all played hard and were really hot and sweaty. I was looking forward to that swim at the waterfront.

Colin was on the Red team. I noticed that he was the only player who wasn't enjoying the game. He had been tagged out twice, and he'd missed an easy catch in the field.

I realized that Colin wasn't very athletic. He had long, skinny arms without any muscles, and he also ran awkwardly.

In the third inning Colin got into an argument with a player on my team about whether a toss had been foul or not. A few minutes later, Colin argued angrily with Larry about a ball that he claimed should have been out.

He and Larry shouted at each other for a few minutes. It was no big deal, a typical sports argument. Larry finally ordered Colin to shut up and get back to the outfield. Colin grudgingly obeyed, and the game continued.

I didn't think about it again. I mean, that kind

of arguing happens all the time in ball games. And there are guys who enjoy the arguments as much as the game.

But then, in the next inning, something strange happened that gave me a really bad feeling and made me stop and wonder just what was going on.

Colin's team came to bat. Colin stepped up to the batter's square and prepared to toss the ball.

Larry was playing the outfield. I was standing nearby, also in the field.

Colin tossed the ball high but not very far.

Larry and I both came running in to get it.

Larry got there first. He picked up the small hard ball on the first bounce, drew back his arm — and then I saw his expression change.

I saw his features tighten in anger. I saw his eyes narrow, his copper-colored eyebrows lower in concentration.

With a loud grunt of effort, Larry heaved the ball as hard as he could.

It struck Colin in the back of the head, making a loud *crack* sound as it hit.

Colin's silver sunglasses went flying in the air.

Colin stopped short and uttered a short, high-pitched cry. His arms flew up as if he'd been shot. Then his knees buckled.

He collapsed in a heap, facedown on the grass. He didn't move.

The ball rolled away over the grass.

I cried out in shock.

Then I saw Larry's expression change again. His eyes opened wide in disbelief. His mouth dropped open in horror.

"No!" he cried. "It slipped! I didn't mean to throw it at him!"

I knew Larry was lying. I had seen the anger on his face before he threw the ball.

I sank down to my knees on the ground as Larry went running toward Colin. I felt dizzy and upset and confused. I had this sick feeling in my stomach.

"The ball slipped!" Larry was yelling. "It just slipped."

Liar, I thought. *Liar. Liar. Liar.*

I forced myself up on my feet and hurried to join the circle of guys around Colin. When I got there, Larry was kneeling over Colin, raising Colin's head off the ground gently with both hands.

Colin's eyes were open wide. He stared up at Larry groggily and uttered low moans.

"Give him room," Larry was shouting. "Give him room." He gazed down at Colin. "The ball slipped. I'm real sorry. The ball slipped."

Colin moaned. His eyes rolled around in his head. Larry pulled off Colin's red bandanna and mopped Colin's forehead with it.

Colin moaned again. His eyes closed.

"Help me carry him to the lodge," Larry instructed two guys from the Red team. "The rest of you guys, get changed for your swim. The waterfront counselor will be waiting for you."

I watched as Larry and the two guys hoisted Colin up and started to carry him toward the lodge. Larry gripped him under the shoulders. The two boys awkwardly took hold of his legs.

The sick feeling in my stomach hadn't gone away. I kept picturing the intense expression of anger on Larry's face as he heaved the ball at the back of Colin's head.

I knew it had been deliberate.

I started to follow them. I don't know why. I guess I was so upset, I wasn't thinking clearly.

They were nearly to the bottom of the hill when I saw Mike catch up to them. He ran alongside Larry, holding his swollen hand.

"Can I come, too?" Mike pleaded. "Someone has to look at my hand. It's really bad, Larry. Please — can I come, too?"

"Yeah. You'd better," I heard Larry reply curtly.

Good, I thought. Finally someone was going to pay some attention to Mike's snakebite wound.

Ignoring the sweat pouring down my forehead, I watched them make their way up the hill to the lodge.

This shouldn't have happened, I thought, suddenly feeling a chill despite the hot sun.

Something is wrong. Something is terribly wrong here.

How was I to know that the horrors were just beginning?

Later that afternoon, Jay and I were writing our letters to our parents. I was feeling pretty upset about things. I kept seeing the angry expression on Larry's face as he heaved the ball at the back of Colin's head.

I wrote about it in my letter, and I also told my mom and dad about how there was no nurse here, and about the Forbidden Bunk.

Jay stopped writing and looked at me from his bunk. He was really sunburned. His cheeks and forehead were bright red.

He scratched his red hair. "We're dropping like flies," he said, gesturing around the nearly empty cabin.

"Yeah," I agreed wistfully. "I hope Colin and Mike are okay." And then I blurted out, "Larry deliberately hit Colin."

"Huh?" Jay stopped scratching his hair and lowered his hand to the bunk. "He *what*?"

"He deliberately threw at Colin's head. I *saw* him," I said, my voice shaky. I wasn't going to tell anyone, but now I was glad I did. It made me feel a little bit better to get it out.

But then I saw that Jay didn't believe me. "That's impossible," he said quietly. "Larry's our counselor. His hand slipped. That's all."

I started to argue when the cabin door opened and Colin entered, with Larry at his side.

"Colin! How *are* you?" I cried.

Jay and I both jumped down from our beds.

"Not bad," Colin replied. He forced a thin smile. I couldn't see his eyes. They were hidden once again behind his silver sunglasses.

"He's still a little wobbly, but he's okay," Larry said cheerfully, holding Colin's arm.

"I'm sort of seeing double," Colin admitted. "I mean, this cabin looks really crowded to me. There are two of each of you."

Jay and I uttered short, uncomfortable laughs.

Larry helped Colin over to his lower bunk. "He'll be just fine in a day or two," Larry told us.

"Yeah. The headache is a little better already," Colin said, gently rubbing the back of his head, then lying down on top of the bedcovers.

"Did you see a doctor?" I asked.

"Uh-uh. Just Uncle Al," Colin replied. "He looked it over and said I'd be fine."

I cast a suspicious glance at Larry, but he turned his back on us and crouched down to search for something in the duffel bag he kept under his bed.

"Where's Mike? Is he okay?" Jay asked Larry.

"Uh-huh," Larry answered without turning around. "He's fine."

"But where is he?" I demanded.

Larry shrugged. "Still at the lodge, I guess. I don't really know."

"But is he coming back?" I insisted.

Larry shoved the bag under his bed and stood up. "Have you guys finished your letters?" he asked. "Hurry and get changed for dinner. You can mail your letters at the lodge."

He started for the door. "Hey, don't forget tonight is Tent Night. You guys are sleeping in a tent tonight."

We all groaned. "But, Larry, it's too cold out!" Jay protested.

Larry ignored him and turned away.

"Hey, Larry, do you have anything I can put on this sunburn?" Jay called after him.

"No," Larry replied, and disappeared out the door.

Jay and I helped Colin up to the lodge. He was still seeing double, and his headache was pretty bad.

The three of us sat at the end of the long table

nearest the window. A strong breeze blew cool air over the table, which felt good on our sunburned skin.

We had some kind of meat with potatoes and gravy for dinner. It wasn't great, but I was so hungry, it didn't matter. Colin didn't have much of an appetite. He picked at the edges of his gray meat.

The mess hall was as noisy as ever. Kids were laughing and shouting to friends across the long tables. At one table, the guys were throwing breadsticks back and forth like javelins.

As usual, the counselors, dressed in their green and white, ate together at a table in the far corner and ignored us campers completely.

The rumor spread that we were going to learn all of the camp songs after dinner. Guys were groaning and complaining about that.

About halfway through dinner, Jay and the boy across the table, a kid named Roger, started horsing around, trying to wrestle a breadstick from each other. Jay pulled hard and won the breadstick — and spilled his entire cup of grape juice on my tan shorts.

"Hey!" I jumped up angrily, staring down as the purple stain spread across the front of my shorts.

"Billy had an accident!" Roger cried out. And everyone laughed.

"Yeah. He purpled in his pants!" Jay added.

Everyone thought that was hilarious. Someone threw a breadstick at me. It bounced off my chest and landed on my dinner plate. More laughter.

The food fight lasted only a few minutes. Then two of the counselors broke it up. I decided I'd better run back to the bunk and change my shorts. As I hurried out, I could hear Jay and Roger calling out jokes about me.

I ran full speed down the hill toward the bunks. I wanted to get back up to the mess hall in time for dessert.

Pushing open the bunk door with my shoulder, I darted across the small room to the dresser and pulled open my drawer.

"Huh?"

To my surprise, I stared into an empty drawer. It had been completely cleaned out.

"What's going on here?" I asked aloud. "Where's my stuff?"

Confused, I took a step back — and realized I had opened the wrong drawer. This wasn't my drawer.

It was Mike's.

I stared for a long while into the empty drawer.

Mike's clothes had all been removed. I turned and looked for his trunk, which had been stacked on its side behind our bunk.

Mike's trunk was gone, too.

Mike wasn't coming back.

*   *   *

I was so upset, I ran back to the mess hall without changing my shorts.

Panting loudly, I made my way to the counselors' table and came up behind Larry. He was talking to the counselor next to him, a fat guy with long, scraggly blond hair. "Larry — Mike's gone!" I cried breathlessly.

Larry didn't turn around. He kept talking to the other counselor as if I weren't there.

I grabbed Larry's shoulder. "Larry — listen!" I cried. "Mike — he's gone!"

Larry turned around slowly, his expression annoyed. "Go back to your table, Billy," he snapped. "This table is for counselors only."

"But what about Mike?" I insisted shrilly. "His stuff is gone. What happened to him? Is he okay?"

"How should I know?" Larry replied impatiently.

"Did they send him home?" I asked, refusing to back away until I had some kind of an answer.

"Yeah. Maybe." Larry shrugged and lowered his gaze. "You spilled something on your shorts."

My heart was pounding so hard, I could feel the blood pulsing at my temples. "You really don't know what happened to Mike?" I asked, feeling defeated.

Larry shook his head. "I'm sure he's fine," he replied, turning back to his pals.

61

"He probably went for a swim," the scraggly haired guy next to him snickered.

Larry and some of the other counselors laughed, too.

I didn't think it was funny. I felt pretty sick. And a little frightened.

Don't the counselors at this camp care what happens to us? I asked myself glumly.

I made my way back to the table. They were passing out chocolate pudding for dessert, but I wasn't hungry.

I told Colin and Jay and Roger about Mike's dresser drawer being cleaned out, and about how Larry pretended he didn't know anything about it. They didn't get as upset about it as I was.

"Uncle Al probably had to send Mike home because of his hand," Colin said quietly, spooning up his pudding. "It was pretty swollen."

"But why wouldn't Larry tell me the truth?" I asked, my stomach still feeling as if I had eaten a giant rock for dinner. "Why did he say he didn't know what happened to Mike?"

"Counselors don't like to talk about bad stuff," Jay said, slapping the top of his pudding with his spoon. "It might give us poor little kids nightmares." He filled his spoon with pudding, tilted it back, and flung a dark gob of pudding onto Roger's forehead.

"Jay — you're dead meat now!" Roger cried,

plunging his spoon into the chocolate goo. He shot a gob of it onto the front of Jay's sleeveless T-shirt.

That started a pudding war that spread down the long table.

There was no more talk about Mike.

After dinner, Uncle Al talked about Tent Night and what a great time we were going to have sleeping in tents tonight. "Just be very quiet so the bears can't find you!" he joked. Some joke.

Then he and the counselors taught us the camp songs. Uncle Al made us sing them over and over until we learned them.

I didn't feel much like singing. But Jay and Roger began making up really gross words to the songs. And pretty soon, a whole bunch of us joined in, singing our own versions of the songs as loudly as we could.

Later, we were all making our way down the hill toward our tents. It was a cool, clear night. A wash of pale stars covered the purple-black sky.

I helped Colin down the hill. He was still seeing double and feeling a little weak.

Jay and Roger walked a few steps ahead of us, shoving each other with their shoulders, first to the left, then to the right.

Suddenly, Jay turned back to Colin and me. "Tonight's the night," he whispered, a devilish grin spreading across his face.

"Huh? Tonight's *what* night?" I demanded.

"*Ssshhh.*" He raised a finger to his lips. "When everyone's asleep, Roger and I are going to go check out the Forbidden Bunk." He turned to Colin. "You with us?"

Colin shook his head sadly. "I don't think I can, Jay."

Walking backward in front of us, Jay locked his eyes on mine. "How about you, Billy? You coming?"

"I — I think I'll stay with Colin," I told him.

I heard Roger mutter something about me being a chicken. Jay looked disappointed. "You're going to miss out," he said.

"That's okay. I'm kind of tired," I said. It was true. I felt so weary after this long day, every muscle ached. Even my hair hurt!

Jay and Roger made whispered plans all the way back to the tent.

At the bottom of the hill, I stopped and gazed up at the Forbidden Bunk. It appeared to lean toward me in the pale starlight. I listened for the familiar howls that seemed to come from inside it. But tonight there was only a heavy silence.

The large plastic tents were lined up in the bunk area. I crawled into ours and lay down on top of my sleeping bag. The ground was really hard. I could see this was going to be a long night.

Jay and Colin were messing around with their sleeping bags at the back of the tent. "It seems weird without Mike here," I said, feeling a sudden chill.

"Now you'll have more room to put your stuff," Jay replied casually. He sat hunched against the tent wall, his expression tense, his eyes on the darkness outside the tent door, which was left open a few inches.

Larry was nowhere in sight. Colin sat quietly. He still wasn't feeling right.

I shifted my weight and stretched out, trying to find a comfortable position. I really wanted to go to sleep. But I knew I wouldn't be able to sleep until after Jay and Roger returned from their adventure.

Time moved slowly. It was cold outside, and the air was heavy and wet inside the tent.

I stared up at the dark plastic tent walls. A bug crawled across my forehead. I squashed it with my hand.

I could hear Jay and Colin whispering behind me, but I couldn't make out their words. Jay snickered nervously.

I must have dozed off. An insistent whispering sound woke me up. It took me a while to realize it was someone whispering outside the tent.

I lifted my head and saw Roger's face peering in. I sat up, alert.

"Wish us luck," Jay whispered.

"Good luck," I whispered back, my voice clogged from sleep.

In the darkness, I saw Jay's large shadowy form crawl quickly to the tent door. He pushed it open, revealing a square of purple sky, then vanished into the darkness.

I shivered. "Let's sneak back to the bunk," I whispered to Colin. "It's too cold out here. And the ground feels like solid rock."

Colin agreed. We both scrambled out of the tent and made our way silently to our nice, warm bunk. Inside, we headed to the window to try to see Jay and Roger.

"They're going to get caught," I whispered. "I just know it."

"They won't get caught," Colin disagreed. "But they won't see anything, either. There's nothing to see up there. It's just a stupid cabin."

Poking my head out the window, I could hear Jay and Roger giggling quietly somewhere out in the dark. The camp was so silent, so eerily silent. I could hear their whispers, their legs brushing through the tall grass.

"They'd better be quiet," Colin muttered, leaning against the window frame. "They're making too much noise."

"They must be up to the hill by now," I whispered. I stuck my head out as far as I could, but I couldn't see them.

Colin started to reply, but the first scream made him stop.

It was a scream of horror that cut through the silent air.

"Oh!" I cried out, and pulled my head in.

"Was that Jay or Roger?" Colin asked, his voice trembling.

The second scream was more terrifying than the first.

Before it died down, I heard animal snarls. Loud and angry. Like an eruption of thunder.

Then I heard Jay's desperate plea: "Help us! Please — somebody help us!"

My heart thudding in my chest, I lurched to the cabin door and pulled it open. The hideous screams still ringing in my ears, I plunged out into the darkness, the dew-covered ground soaking my bare feet.

"Jay — where are you?" I heard myself calling, but I didn't recognize my shrill, frightened voice.

And then I saw a dark form running toward me, running bent over, arms outstretched.

"Jay!" I cried. "What — *is* it? What *happened*?"

He ran up to me, still bent forward, his face twisted in horror, his eyes wide and unblinking. His bushy hair appeared to stand straight up.

"It — it got Roger," he moaned, his chest heaving as he struggled to straighten up.

68

"What did?" I demanded.

"What was it?" Colin asked, right behind me.

"I — I don't know!" Jay stammered, shutting his eyes tight. "It — it tore Roger to pieces."

Jay uttered a loud sob. Then he opened his eyes and spun around in terror. "Here it comes!" he shrieked. "Now it's coming after *us!*"

In the pale starlight, I saw Jay's eyes roll up in his head. His knees collapsed, and he began to slump to the ground.

I grabbed him before he fell and dragged him into the cabin. Colin slammed the door behind us.

Once inside, Jay recovered slowly. The three of us froze in place and listened hard. I was still holding on to Jay's heaving shoulders. He was as pale as a bedsheet, and his breath came out in short, frightened moans.

We listened.

Silence.

The air hung frozen and still.

Nothing moved.

No footsteps. No animal approaching.

Just Jay's frightened moans and the pounding of my heart.

And then, somewhere far in the distance, I heard the howl. Soft and low at first, then rising on the wind. A howl that chilled my blood and made me cry out.

"It's Sabre!"

"Don't let it get me!" Jay shrieked, covering his face with his hands. He dropped to his knees on the cabin floor. "Don't let it get me!"

I raised my eyes to Colin, who was huddled against the wall, away from the window. "We have to get Larry," I managed to choke out. "We have to get help."

"But how?" Colin demanded in a trembling voice.

"Don't let it get me!" Jay repeated, crumpled on the floor.

"It isn't coming here," I told him, trying to sound certain, trying to sound soothing. "We're okay inside the bunk, Jay. It isn't coming here."

"But it got Roger and —" Jay started. His entire body convulsed in a shudder of terror.

Thinking about Roger, I felt a stab of fear in my chest.

Was it really true? Was it true that Roger had been attacked by some kind of creature? That he'd been slashed to pieces?

I'd heard the screams from the hillside. Two bloodcurdling screams.

They'd been so loud, so horrifying. Hadn't anyone else in camp heard them, too? Hadn't any other kids heard Roger's cries? Hadn't any counselors heard?

71

I froze in place and listened.

Silence. The whisper of the breeze rustling the tree leaves.

No voices. No cries of alarm. No hurried footsteps.

I turned back toward the others. Colin had helped Jay to his bunk. "Where can Larry be?" Colin asked. His eyes, for once not hidden behind the silver sunglasses, showed real fear.

"Where can *everyone* be?" I asked, crossing my arms over my chest and starting to pace back and forth in the small space between the beds. "There isn't a sound out there."

I saw Jay's eyes go wide with horror. He was staring at the open window. "The creature —" he cried. "Here it comes! It's coming through the window!"

All three of us gaped in horror at the open window.

But no creature jumped in.

As I stared, frozen in the center of the cabin, I could see only darkness and a fringe of pale stars.

Outside in the trees, crickets started up a shrill clatter. There was no other sound.

Poor Jay was so frightened and upset, he was seeing things.

Somehow Colin and I got him a little calmed down. We made him take off his sneakers and lie down on his bed. And we covered him up with three blankets to help him to stop trembling.

Colin and I wanted to run for help. But we were too frightened to go outside.

The three of us were up all night. Larry never showed up.

Except for the crickets and the brush of the wind through the trees, the camp was silent.

I think I must have finally dozed off just before dawn. I had strange nightmares about fires and people trying to run away.

I was awakened by Colin shaking me hard. "Breakfast," he said hoarsely. "Hurry. We're late."

I sat up groggily. "Where's Larry?"

"He never showed," Colin replied, motioning to Larry's unused bunk.

"We've got to find him! We've got to tell him what happened!" Jay cried, hurrying to the cabin door with his sneakers untied.

Colin and I stumbled after him, both of us only half awake. It was a cool, gray morning. The sun was trying hard to poke through high white clouds.

The three of us stopped halfway up the hill to the mess hall. Reluctantly, our eyes searched the ground around the Forbidden Bunk.

I don't know what I expected to see. But there was no sign of Roger.

No sign of any struggle. No dried blood on the ground. The tall grass wasn't bent or matted down.

"Weird," I heard Jay mutter, shaking his head. "That's weird."

I tugged his arm to get him moving, and we hurried the rest of the way up to the lodge.

The mess hall was as noisy as ever. Kids were laughing and shouting to each other. It all seemed perfectly normal. I guessed that no one had made an announcement about Roger yet.

Some kids called to Colin and me. But we ignored them and searched for Roger, moving quickly through the aisles between the tables.

No sign of him.

I had a heavy, queasy feeling in my stomach as we hurried to the counselors' table in the corner.

Larry glanced up from a big plate of scrambled eggs and bacon as the three of us advanced on him.

"What happened to Roger?"

"Is he okay?"

"Where were you last night?"

"Roger and I were attacked."

"We were afraid to go find you."

All three of us bombarded Larry at once.

His face was filled with confusion, and he raised both hands to silence us. "Whoa," he said. "Take a breath, guys. What are you talking about?"

"About Roger!" Jay screamed, his face turning bright red. "The creature — it jumped on him. And — and —"

Larry glanced at the other counselors at the table, who looked as confused as he did. "Creature? What creature?" Larry demanded.

"It attacked Roger!" Jay screamed. "It was coming after me and —"

Larry stared up at Jay. "Someone was attacked? I don't think so, Jay." He turned to the counselor next to him, a pudgy boy named Derek. "Did you hear anything in your area?"

Derek shook his head.

"Isn't Roger in your group?" Larry asked Derek.

Derek shook his head. "Not in *my* group."

"But Roger —" Jay insisted.

"We didn't get any report about any attack," Larry said, interrupting. "If a camper was attacked by a bear or something, we'd hear about it."

"And we'd hear the noise," Derek offered. "You know. Screams or something."

"I heard screams," I told them.

"We both heard screams," Colin added quickly. "And Jay came running back, crying for help."

"Well, why didn't anyone else hear it?" Larry demanded, turning his gaze on Jay. His expression changed. "Where did this happen? When?" he asked suspiciously.

Jay's face darkened to a deeper red. "After lights-out," he admitted. "Roger and I went up to the Forbidden Bunk, and —"

"Are you sure it wasn't a bear?" Derek interrupted. "Some bears were spotted downriver yesterday afternoon."

"It was a *creature*!" Jay screamed angrily.

"You shouldn't have been out," Larry said, shaking his head.

"Why won't you listen to me?" Jay screamed. "Roger was attacked. This big thing jumped on him and —"

"We would have heard something," Derek said calmly, glancing at Larry.

"Yeah," Larry agreed. "The counselors were all up here at the lodge. We would've heard any screams."

"But, Larry — you've got to check it out!" I cried. "Jay isn't making it up. It really happened!"

"Okay, okay," Larry replied, raising his hands as if surrendering. "I'll go ask Uncle Al about it, okay?"

"Hurry," Jay insisted. "Please!"

"I'll ask Uncle Al after breakfast," Larry said, turning back to his eggs and bacon. "I'll see you guys at morning swim later. I'll report what Uncle Al says."

"But, Larry —" Jay pleaded.

"I'll ask Uncle Al," Larry said firmly. "If anything happened last night, he'll know about it." He raised a strip of bacon to his mouth and chewed on it. "I think you just had a bad nightmare or something," he continued, eyeing Jay suspiciously. "But I'll let you know what Uncle Al says."

"It wasn't a nightmare!" Jay cried shrilly. Larry

turned his back on us and continued eating his breakfast. "Don't you *care*?" Jay screamed at him. "Don't you *care* what happens to us?"

I saw that a lot of kids had stopped eating their breakfast to gawk at us. I pulled Jay away and tried to get him to go to our table. But he insisted on searching the entire mess hall again. "I know Roger *isn't* here," he insisted. "He — he *can't* be!"

For the second time, the three of us made our way up and down the aisles between the tables, studying every face.

One thing was for sure: Roger was nowhere to be seen.

The sun burned through the high clouds just as we reached the waterfront for morning swim. The air was still cool. The thick, leafy shrubs along the riverbank glistened wetly in the white glare of sunlight.

I dropped my towel under a bush and turned to the gently flowing green water. "I'll bet it's cold this morning," I said to Colin, who was retying the string on his swim trunks.

"I just want to go back to the bunk and go to sleep," Colin said, plucking at a knot. He wasn't seeing double any longer, but he was tired from being up all night.

Several guys were already wading into the river. They were complaining about the cold water, splashing each other, shoving each other forward.

"Where's Larry?" Jay demanded breathlessly, pushing his way through the clump of shrubs to get to us. His red hair was a mess, half of it standing straight up on the side of his head. His eyes were red-rimmed and bloodshot.

"Where's Larry? He promised he'd be here," Jay said, frantically searching the waterfront.

"Here I am." The three of us spun around as Larry appeared from the bushes behind us. He was wearing baggy green Camp Nightmoon swim trunks.

"Well?" Jay demanded. "What did Uncle Al say? About Roger?"

Larry's expression was serious. His eyes locked on Jay's. "Uncle Al and I went all around the Forbidden Bunk," he told Jay. "There wasn't any attack there. There couldn't have been."

"But it — it got Roger," Jay cried shrilly. "It slashed him. I saw it!"

Larry shook his head, his eyes still burning into Jay's. "That's the other thing," he said softly. "Uncle Al and I went up to the office and checked the records, Jay. And there *is* no camper here this year named Roger. Not a first name or a middle name. No Roger. No Roger at all."

Jay's mouth dropped open, and he uttered a low gasp.

The three of us stared in disbelief at Larry, letting this startling news sink in.

"Someone's made a mistake," Jay said finally, his voice trembling with emotion. "We searched the mess hall for him, Larry. And he's gone. Roger isn't here."

"He never *was* here," Larry said without any emotion at all.

"I — I just don't believe this!" Jay cried.

"How about a swim, guys?" Larry said, motioning to the water.

"Well, what do *you* think?" I demanded of Larry. I couldn't believe he was being so calm about this. "What do *you* think happened last night?"

Larry shrugged. "I don't know what to think," he replied, his eyes on the cluster of swimmers farthest from the shore. "Maybe you guys are trying to pull a weird joke on me."

"Huh? Is *that* what you think?" Jay cried. "That it's a *joke*?!"

Larry shrugged again. "Swim time, guys. Get some exercise, okay?"

Jay started to say more, but Larry quickly turned and went running into the green water. He took four or five running steps off the shore, then dived, pulling himself quickly through the water, taking long, steady strokes.

"I'm not going in," Jay insisted angrily. "I'm going back to the bunk." His face was bright red. His chin was trembling. I could see that he was about to cry. He turned and began running through the bushes, dragging his towel along the ground.

"Hey, wait up!" Colin went running after him.

I stood there trying to decide what to do. I didn't want to follow Jay to the bunk. There wasn't anything I could do to help him.

Maybe a cold swim will make me feel better, I thought.

Maybe nothing *will make me feel better*, I told myself glumly.

I stared out at the other guys in the water. Larry and another counselor were setting up a race. I could hear them discussing what kind of stroke should be used.

They all seem to be having a great time, I thought, watching them line up.

So why aren't I?

Why have I been so frightened and unhappy since I arrived here? Why don't the other campers see how weird and frightening this place is?

I shook my head, unable to answer my questions.

I need a swim, I decided.

I took a step toward the water.

But someone reached out from the bushes and grabbed me roughly from behind.

I started to scream out in protest.

But my attacker quickly clamped a hand over my mouth to silence me.

I tried to pull away, but I'd been caught off guard.

As the hands tugged me, I lost my balance and I was pulled back into the bushes.

Is this a joke? What's going on? I wondered.

Suddenly, as I tried to tug myself free, the hands let go.

I went sailing headfirst into a clump of fat green leaves.

It took me a long moment to pull myself up. Then I spun around to face my attacker.

"Dawn!" I cried.

"*Ssshhh!*" She leaped forward and clamped a hand over my mouth again. "Duck down," she whispered urgently. "They'll see you."

I obediently ducked behind the low bush. She let go of me again and moved back. She was wearing a blue one-piece bathing suit. It was wet. Her blond hair was also wet, dripping down onto her bare shoulders.

"Dawn — what are you *doing* here?" I whispered, settling onto my knees.

Before Dawn could reply, another figure in a bathing suit moved quickly from the bushes, crouching low. It was Dawn's friend Dori.

"We swam over. Early this morning," Dori whispered, nervously pushing at her curly red hair. "We waited here. In the bushes."

"But it's not allowed," I said, unable to hide my confusion. "If you're caught —"

"We had to talk to you," Dawn interrupted, raising her head to peek over the top of the bushes, then quickly ducking back down.

"We decided to risk it," Dori added.

"What — what's wrong?" I stammered. A red-and-black bug crawled up my shoulder. I brushed it away.

"The girls' camp. It's a nightmare," Dori whispered.

"Everyone calls it *Camp Nightmare* instead of Camp Nightmoon," Dawn added. "Strange things have been happening."

"Huh?" I gaped at her. Not far from us in the water, I could hear the shouts and splashes of the swim race beginning. "What kinds of strange things?"

"Scary things," Dori replied, her expression solemn.

"Girls have disappeared," Dawn told me. "Just vanished from sight."

"And no one seems to care," Dori added in a trembling whisper.

"I don't believe it!" I uttered. "The same thing has happened here. At the boys' camp." I swallowed hard. "Remember Mike?"

Both girls nodded.

"Mike disappeared," I told them. "They removed his stuff, and he just disappeared."

"It's unbelievable," Dori said. "Three girls are gone from our camp."

"They announced that one was attacked by a bear," Dawn whispered.

"What about the other two?" I asked.

"Just gone," Dawn replied, the words catching in her throat.

I could hear whistles blowing in the water. The race had ended. Another one was being organized.

The sun disappeared once again behind high white clouds. Shadows lengthened and grew darker.

I told them quickly about Roger and Jay and the attack at the Forbidden Bunk. They listened in openmouthed silence. "Just like at our camp," Dawn said.

"We have to do something," Dori said heatedly.

"We have to get together. The boys and the girls," Dawn whispered, peering once again over the tops of the leaves. "We have to make a plan."

"You mean to escape?" I asked, not really understanding.

The two girls nodded. "We can't stay here," Dawn said grimly. "Every day another girl disappears. And the counselors act as if nothing is happening."

"I think they *want* us to get killed or something," Dori added with emotion.

"Have you written to your parents?" I asked.

"We write every day," Dori replied. "But we haven't heard from them."

I suddenly realized that I hadn't received any mail from my parents, either. They had both promised to write every day. But I had been at camp for nearly a week, and I hadn't received a single piece of mail.

"Visitors Day is next week," I said. "Our parents will be here. We can tell them everything."

"It may be too late," Dawn said grimly.

"Everyone is so scared!" Dori declared. "I haven't slept in two nights. I hear these horrible screams outside every night."

Another whistle blew, closer to shore. I could hear the swimmers returning. Morning swim was ending.

"I — I don't know what to say," I told them. "You've got to be careful. Don't get caught."

"We'll swim back to the girls' camp when everyone has left," Dawn said. "But we have to meet again, Billy. We have to get more guys together. You know. Maybe if we all get organized . . ." Her voice trailed off.

"There's something bad going on at this camp," Dori said with a shiver, narrowing her eyes. "Something evil."

"I — I know," I agreed. I could hear boys' voices now. Close by. Just on the other side of the leafy bushes. "I've got to go."

"We'll try to meet here again the day after tomorrow," Dawn whispered. "Be careful, Billy."

"*You* be careful," I whispered. "Don't get caught."

They slipped back, deeper in the bushes.

Crouching low, I made my way away from the shore. When I was past the clump of bushes, I stood up and began to run. I couldn't wait to tell Colin and Jay about what the girls had said.

I felt frightened and excited at the same time. I thought maybe it would make Jay feel a little better to know that the same kinds of horrible things were happening across the river at the girls' camp.

Halfway to the bunks, I had an idea. I stopped and turned toward the lodge.

I suddenly remembered seeing a pay phone on the wall on the side of the building. Someone had told me that phone was the only one campers were allowed to use.

I'll call Mom and Dad, I decided.

Why hadn't I thought of it before?

I can call my parents, I realized, *and tell them everything. I can ask them to come and get me. And they could get Jay, Colin, Dawn, and Dori, too.*

Behind me, I saw my group heading toward the scratchball field, their swimming towels slung over their shoulders. I wondered if anyone had noticed that I was missing.

Jay and Colin were missing, too, I told myself. Larry and the others probably think I'm with them.

I watched them trooping across the tall grass in twos and threes. Then I turned and started jogging up the hill toward the lodge.

The idea of calling home had cheered me up already.

I was so eager to hear my parents' voices, so eager to tell them the strange things that were happening here.

Would they believe me?

Of *course* they would. My parents always believed me. Because they trusted me.

As I ran up the hill, the dark pay phone came into view on the white lodge wall. I started to run at full speed. I wanted to *fly* to the phone.

I hope Mom and Dad are home, I thought. *They've got to be home.*

I was panting loudly as I reached the wall. I lowered my hands to my knees and crouched there for a moment, waiting to catch my breath.

Then I reached up to take the receiver down. And gasped.

The pay phone was plastic. Just a stage prop. A phony.

It was a thin sheet of molded plastic held to the wall by a nail, made to look just like a telephone.

It wasn't real. It was a fake.

They don't want us to call out, I thought with a sudden chill.

My heart thudding, my head spinning in bitter disappointment, I turned away from the wall — and bumped right into Uncle Al.

"Billy — what are you doing up here?" Uncle Al asked. He was wearing baggy green camp shorts and a sleeveless white T-shirt that revealed his meaty pink arms. He carried a brown clipboard filled with papers. "Where are you supposed to be?"

"I . . . uh . . . wanted to make a phone call," I stammered, taking a step back. "I wanted to call my parents."

He eyed me suspiciously and fingered his yellow mustache. "Really?"

"Yeah. Just to say hi," I told him. "But the phone —"

Uncle Al followed my gaze to the plastic phone. He chuckled. "Someone put that up as a joke," he said, grinning at me. "Did it fool you?"

"Yeah," I admitted, feeling my face grow hot. I raised my eyes to his. "Where is the real phone?"

His grin faded. His expression turned serious. "No phone," he replied sharply. "Campers aren't allowed to call out. It's a rule, Billy."

"Oh." I didn't know what to say.

"Are you really homesick?" Uncle Al asked softly.

I nodded.

"Well, go write your mom and dad a long letter," he said. "It'll make you feel a lot better."

"Okay," I said. I didn't think it *would* make me feel better. But I wanted to get away from Uncle Al.

He raised his clipboard and gazed at it. "Where are you supposed to be now?" he asked.

"Scratchball, I think," I replied. "I didn't feel too well, see. So I —"

"And when is your canoe trip?" he asked, not listening to me. He flipped through the sheets of paper on the clipboard, glancing over them quickly.

"Canoe trip?" I hadn't heard about any canoe trip.

"Tomorrow," he said, answering his own question. "Your group goes tomorrow. Are you excited?" He lowered his eyes to mine.

"I — I didn't really know about it," I confessed.

"Lots of fun!" he exclaimed enthusiastically. "The river doesn't look like much up here. But it gets pretty exciting a few miles down. You'll find yourself in some good rapids."

He squeezed my shoulder briefly. "You'll enjoy it," he said, grinning. "Everyone always enjoys the canoe trip."

"Great," I said. I tried to sound a little excited, but my voice came out flat and uncertain.

Uncle Al gave me a wave with his clipboard and headed around toward the front of the lodge, taking long strides. I stood watching him till he disappeared around the corner of the building. Then I made my way down the hill to the bunk.

I found Colin and Jay on the grass at the side of the cabin. Colin had his shirt off and was sprawled on his back, his hands behind his head. Jay sat cross-legged beside him, nervously pulling up long, slender strands of grass, then tossing them down.

"Come inside," I told them, glancing around to make sure no one else could hear.

They followed me into the cabin. I closed the door.

"What's up?" Colin asked, dropping onto his bunk. He picked up his red bandanna and twisted it in his hands.

I told them about Dawn and Dori and what they had reported about the girls' camp.

Colin and Jay both reacted with shock.

"They really swam over here and waited for you?" Jay asked.

I nodded. "They think we have to get organized or escape or something," I said.

"They could get in big trouble if they get caught," Jay said thoughtfully.

"We're all in big trouble," I told him. "We have to get *out*!"

"Visitors Day is next week," Colin muttered.

"I'm going to write my parents right now," I said, pulling out the case from under my bunk where I kept my paper and pens. "I'm going to tell them I *have* to come home on Visitors Day."

"I guess I will, too," Jay said, tapping his fingers nervously against the bunk frame.

"Me, too," Colin agreed. "It's just too . . . weird here!"

I pulled out a couple of sheets of paper and sat down on the bed to write. "Dawn and Dori were really scared," I told them.

"So am I," Jay admitted.

I started to write my letter. I wrote *Dear Mom and Dad, HELP!* then stopped. I raised my eyes across the cabin to Jay and Colin. "Do you guys know about the canoe trip tomorrow?" I asked.

They stared back at me, their expressions surprised.

"Whoa!" Colin declared. "A three-mile hike this afternoon, and a canoe trip tomorrow?"

It was my turn to be surprised. "Hike? What hike?"

"Aren't you coming on it?" Jay asked.

"You know that really tall counselor? Frank? The one who wears the yellow cap?" Colin asked. "He told Jay and me we're going on a three-mile hike after lunch."

"No one told me," I replied, chewing on the end of my pen.

"Maybe you're not in the hike group," Jay said.

"You'd better ask Frank at lunch," Colin suggested. "Maybe he couldn't find you. Maybe you're supposed to come, too."

I groaned. "Who wants to go on a three-mile hike in this heat?"

Colin and Jay both shrugged.

"Frank said we'd really like it," Colin told me, knotting and unknotting the red bandanna.

"I just want to get out of here," I said, returning to my letter.

I wrote quickly, intensely. I wanted to tell my parents all the frightening, strange things that had happened. I wanted to make them see why I couldn't stay at Camp Nightmoon.

I had written nearly a page and a half, and I was up to the part where Jay and Roger went out to explore the Forbidden Bunk, when Larry burst in. "You guys taking the day off?" he asked, his eyes going from one of us to the other. "You on vacation or something?"

"Just hanging out," Jay replied.

I folded up my letter and started to tuck it under my pillow. I didn't want Larry to see it. I realized I didn't trust Larry at all. I had no reason to.

"What are *you* doing, Billy?" he asked suspiciously, his eyes stopping on the letter I was shoving under the pillow.

"Just writing home," I replied softly.

"You homesick or something?" he asked, a grin spreading across his face.

"Maybe," I muttered.

"Well, it's lunchtime, guys," he announced. "Let's hustle, okay?"

We all climbed out of our bunks.

"Jay and Colin are going on a hike with Frank this afternoon, I heard," Larry said. "Lucky guys." He turned and started out the door.

"Larry!" I called to him. "Hey, Larry — what about me? Am I supposed to go on the hike, too?"

"Not today," he called back.

"But why not?" I said.

But Larry disappeared out the door.

I turned back to my two bunk mates. "Lucky guys!" I teased them.

They both growled back at me in reply. Then we headed up the hill to lunch.

They served pizza for lunch, which is usually my favorite. But today, the pizza was cold and tasted like cardboard, and the cheese stuck to the roof of my mouth.

I wasn't really hungry.

I kept thinking about Dawn and Dori, how frightened they were, how desperate. I wondered when I'd see them again. I wondered if they would swim over and hide at the boys' camp again before Visitors Day.

After lunch, Frank came by our table to pick up Jay and Colin. I asked him if I was supposed to come, too.

"You weren't on the list, Billy," he said, scratching at a mosquito bite on his neck. "I can only take two at a time, you know? The trail gets a little dangerous."

"Dangerous?" Jay asked, climbing up from the table.

Frank grinned at him. "You're a big strong guy," he told Jay. "You'll do okay."

I watched Frank lead Colin and Jay out of the mess hall. Our table was empty now, except for a couple of blond-haired guys I didn't know who were arm wrestling down at the end near the wall.

I pushed my tray away and stood up. I wanted to go back to the bunk and finish the letter to my parents. But as I took a few steps toward the door, I felt a hand on my shoulder.

I turned to see Larry grinning down at me. "Tennis tournament," he said.

"Huh?" I reacted with surprise.

"Billy, you're representing Bunk Four in the tennis tournament," Larry said. "Didn't you see the lineup? It was posted on the announcements board."

"But I'm a terrible tennis player!" I protested.

"We're counting on you," Larry replied. "Get a racket and get your bod to the courts!"

I spent the afternoon playing tennis. I beat a little kid in straight sets. I had the feeling he had never held a tennis racket before. Then I lost a long, hard-fought match to one of the blond-haired boys who'd been arm wrestling at lunch.

I was drowning in sweat, and every muscle in my body ached when the match was over. I headed to the waterfront for a refreshing swim.

Then I returned to the bunk, changed into jeans and a green-and-white Camp Nightmoon T-shirt, and finished my letter to my parents.

It was nearly dinnertime. Jay and Colin weren't back from their hike yet. I decided to go up to the lodge and mail my letter. As I headed up the hill, I saw clusters of kids hurrying to their bunks to change for dinner. But no sign of my two bunk mates.

Holding the letter tightly, I headed around to the back of the lodge building, where the camp office was located. The door was wide open, so I walked in. A young woman was usually behind the counter to answer questions and to take the letters to be mailed.

"Anyone here?" I called, leaning over the counter and peering into the tiny back room, which was dark.

No reply.

"Hi. Anyone here?" I repeated, clutching the envelope.

No. The office was empty.

Disappointed, I started to leave. Then I glimpsed the large burlap bag on the floor just inside the tiny back room.

The mailbag!

I decided to put my letter in the bag with the others to be mailed. I slipped around the counter and into the back room and crouched down to put my envelope into the bag.

To my surprise, the mailbag was stuffed full with letters. As I pulled the bag open and started to shove my letter inside, a bunch of letters fell out onto the floor.

I started to scoop them up when a letter caught my eye.

It was one of mine. Addressed to my parents.

One I had written yesterday.

"Weird," I muttered aloud.

Bending over the bag, I reached in and pulled out a big handful of letters. I sifted through them quickly. I found a letter Colin had written.

I pulled out another pile.

And my eyes fell upon two other letters I had written nearly a week ago when I first arrived at camp.

I stared at them, feeling a cold chill run down my back.

All of our letters, all of the letters we had written since the first day of camp, were here. In this mailbag.

None of them had been mailed.

We couldn't call home.

And we couldn't *write* home.

Frantically, my hands trembling, I began shoving the envelopes back into the mailbag.

What is going on here? I wondered. *What is going on?*

By the time I got into the mess hall, Uncle Al was finishing the evening announcements. I slid into my seat, hoping I hadn't missed anything important.

I expected to see Jay and Colin across the table from me. But their places on the bench were empty.

That's strange, I thought, still shaken from my discovery about the mailbag. *They should be back by now.*

I wanted to tell them about the mail. I wanted to share the news that our parents weren't getting any of the letters we wrote.

And we weren't getting any of theirs.

The camp had to be keeping our mail from us, I suddenly realized.

Colin and Jay — where are you?

The fried chicken was greasy, and the mashed potatoes were lumpy and tasted like paste. As I forced the food down, I kept turning to glance at the mess hall door, expecting to see my two bunk mates.

But they didn't show up.

A heavy feeling of dread formed in my stomach. Through the mess hall window, I could see that it was already dark outside.

Where could they be?

A three-mile hike and back shouldn't take this many hours.

I pulled myself up and made my way to the counselors' table in the corner. Larry was having a loud argument about sports with two of the other counselors. They were shouting and gesturing with their hands.

Frank's chair was empty.

"Larry, did Frank get back?" I interrupted their discussion.

Larry turned, a startled expression on his face. "Frank?" He motioned to the empty chair at the table. "Guess not."

"He took Jay and Colin on the hike," I said. "Shouldn't they be back by now?"

Larry shrugged. "Beats me." He returned to his argument, leaving me standing there staring at Frank's empty chair.

After the trays had been cleared, we pushed the tables and benches against the wall and had indoor relay races. Everyone seemed to be having a great time. The shouts and cheers echoed off the high-raftered ceiling.

I was too worried about Jay and Colin to enjoy the games.

Maybe they decided to camp out overnight, I told myself.

But I had seen them leave, and I knew they hadn't taken any tents or sleeping bags or other overnight supplies.

So where *were* they?

The games ended a little before lights-out. As I followed the crowd to the door, Larry appeared beside me. "We're leaving early tomorrow," he said. "First thing."

"Huh?" I didn't understand what he meant.

"The canoe trip. I'm the canoe counselor. I'll be taking you guys," he explained, seeing my confusion.

"Oh. Okay," I replied without enthusiasm. I was so worried about Jay and Colin, I'd nearly forgotten about the canoe trip.

"Right after breakfast," Larry said. "Wear a bathing suit. Bring a change of clothes. Meet me at the waterfront." He hurried back to help the other counselors pull the tables into place.

"After breakfast," I muttered. I wondered if Jay and Colin were also coming on the canoe trip. I had forgotten to ask Larry.

I headed quickly down the dark hill. The dew had already fallen, and the tall grass was slippery and wet. Halfway down, I could see the dark outline of the Forbidden Bunk, hunched forward as if preparing to strike.

Forcing myself to look away, I jogged the rest of the way to Bunk 4.

To my surprise, I could see through the window that someone was moving around inside.

Colin and Jay are back! I thought.

Eagerly, I pushed open the door and burst inside. "Hey — where've you guys been?" I cried.

I stopped short. And gasped.

Two strangers stared back at me.

One was sitting on the edge of Colin's bunk, pulling off his sneakers. The other was leaning over the dresser, pulling a T-shirt from one of the drawers.

"Hi. You in here?" the boy at the dresser stood up straight, his eyes studying me. He had very short black hair and a gold stud in one ear.

I swallowed hard. "Am I in the wrong bunk? Is this Bunk Four?"

They both stared at me, confused.

I saw that the other boy, the one in Colin's bunk, also had black hair, but his was long and scraggly and fell over his forehead. "Yeah. This is Bunk Four," he said.

"We're new," the short-haired boy added. "I'm Tommy, and he's Chris. We just started today."

"Hi," I said uncertainly. "My name's Billy." My

heart was pounding like a tom-tom in my chest. "Where're Colin and Jay?"

"Who?" Chris asked. "They told us this bunk was mostly empty."

"Well, Colin and Jay —" I started.

"We just arrived. We don't know anyone," Tommy interrupted. He pushed the drawer shut.

"But that's Jay's drawer," I said, bewildered, pointing. "What did you do with Jay's stuff?"

Tommy gazed back at me in surprise. "The drawer was empty," he replied.

"Almost all the drawers were empty," Chris added, tossing his sneakers to the floor. "Except for the bottom two drawers."

"That's my stuff," I said, my head spinning. "But Colin and Jay — their stuff was here," I insisted.

"The whole cabin was empty," Tommy said. "Maybe your friends got moved."

"Maybe," I said weakly. I sat down on the lower bunk beneath my bed. My legs felt shaky. A million thoughts were whirring through my mind, all of them frightening.

"This is weird," I said aloud.

"It's not a bad bunk," Chris said, pulling down his blanket and settling in. "Kind of cozy."

"How long you staying at camp?" Tommy asked, pulling on an oversized white T-shirt. "All summer?"

"No!" I exclaimed with a shudder. "I'm not staying!" I sputtered. "I mean . . . I mean . . . I'm leaving. On . . . uh . . . I'm leaving on Visitors Day next week."

Chris flashed Tommy a surprised glance. "Huh? When are you leaving?" he asked again.

"On Visitors Day," I repeated. "When my parents come up for Visitors Day."

"But didn't you hear Uncle Al's announcement before dinner?" Tommy asked, staring hard at me. "Visitors Day has been canceled!"

I drifted in and out of a troubled sleep that night. Even with the blanket pulled up to my chin, I felt chilled and afraid.

It felt so weird to have two strange guys in the bunk, sleeping where Jay and Colin had slept. I was worried about my missing friends.

What had happened to them? Why hadn't they come back?

As I tossed restlessly in my top bunk, I heard howls off in the distance. Animal cries, probably coming from the Forbidden Bunk. Long, frightening howls carried by the wind into our open bunk windows.

At one point, I thought I heard kids screaming. I sat up straight, suddenly alert, and listened.

Had I dreamed the frightful shrieks? I was so scared and confused, it was impossible to tell what was real and what was a nightmare.

It took hours to fall back to sleep.

I awoke to a gray, overcast morning, the air heavy and cold. Pulling on swim trunks and a T-shirt, I raced to the lodge to find Larry. I had to find out what had happened to Jay and Colin.

I searched everywhere for him without success. Larry wasn't at breakfast. None of the other counselors admitted to knowing anything. Frank, the counselor who had taken my two friends on the hike, was also not there.

I finally found Larry at the waterfront, preparing a long metal canoe for our river trip. "Larry — where are they?" I cried out breathlessly.

He gazed up at me, holding an armload of canoe paddles. His expression turned to bewilderment. "Huh? Chris and Tommy? They'll be here soon."

"No!" I cried, grabbing his arm. "Jay and Colin! Where are they? What happened to them, Larry? You've *got* to tell me!"

I gripped his arm tightly. I was gasping for breath. I could feel the blood pulsing at my temples. "You've got to tell me!" I repeated shrilly.

He pulled away from me and let the paddles fall beside the canoe. "I don't know anything about them," he replied quietly.

"But, Larry!"

"Really, I don't," he insisted in the same quiet voice. His expression softened. He placed a hand on my trembling shoulder. "Tell you what, Billy," he said, staring hard into my eyes. "I'll ask Uncle Al about it after our trip, okay? I'll find out for you. When we get back."

I stared back at him, trying to decide if he was being honest.

I couldn't tell. His eyes were as calm and cold as marbles.

He leaned forward and pushed the canoe into the shallow river water. "Here. Take one of those life preservers," he said, pointing to a pile of blue rubber vests behind me. "Strap it on. Then get in."

I did as he instructed. I saw that I had no choice.

Chris and Tommy came running up to us a few seconds later. They obediently followed Larry's instructions and strapped on the life preserver vests.

A few minutes later, the four of us were seated cross-legged inside the long, slender canoe, drifting slowly away from the shore.

The sky was still charcoal gray, the sun hidden behind hovering dark clouds. The canoe bumped over the choppy river water. The current was stronger than I had realized. We began to pick up speed. The low trees and shrubs along the river-bank slid past rapidly.

Larry sat facing us in the front of the canoe. He

demonstrated how to paddle as the river carried us away.

He watched carefully, a tight frown on his face, as the three of us struggled to pick up the rhythm he was showing us. Then, when we finally seemed to catch on, Larry grinned and carefully turned around, gripping the sides of the canoe as he shifted his position.

"The sun is trying to come out," he said, his voice muffled in the strong breeze over the rippling water.

I glanced up. The sky looked darker than before.

He stayed with his back to us, facing forward, allowing the three of us to do the paddling. I had never paddled a canoe before. It was harder than I'd imagined. But as I fell into the rhythm of it with Tommy and Chris, I began to enjoy it.

Dark water smacked against the prow of the canoe, sending up splashes of white froth. The current grew stronger, and we picked up speed. The air was still cold, but the steady work of rowing warmed me. After a while, I realized I was sweating.

We rowed past tangles of yellow- and gray-trunked trees. The river suddenly divided in two, and we shifted our paddles to take the left branch. Larry began paddling again, working to keep us off the tall rocks that jutted between the river branches.

The canoe bobbed up and slapped down. Bobbed up and slapped down. Cold water poured over the sides.

The sky darkened even more. I wondered if it was about to storm.

As the river widened, the current grew rapid and strong. I realized we didn't really need to paddle. The river was doing most of the work.

The river sloped down. Wide swirls of frothing white water made the canoe leap and bounce.

"Here come the rapids!" Larry shouted, cupping his hands around his mouth so we could hear him. "Hang on! It gets pretty wild!"

I felt a tremor of fear as a wave of icy water splashed over me. The canoe rose up on a shelf of white water, then hit hard as it landed.

I could hear Tommy and Chris laughing excitedly behind me.

Another icy wave rolled over the canoe, startling me. I cried out and nearly let go of my paddle.

Tommy and Chris laughed again.

I took a deep breath and held on tightly to the paddle, struggling to keep up the rhythm.

"Hey, look!" Larry cried suddenly.

To my astonishment, he climbed to his feet. He

leaned forward, pointing to the swirling white water.

"Look at those fish!"

As he leaned down, the canoe was jarred by a powerful rush of current. The canoe spun to the right.

I saw the startled look on Larry's face as he lost his balance. His arms shot forward, and he plunged headfirst into the tossing waters.

"Noooooo!" I screamed.

I glanced back at Tommy and Chris, who had stopped paddling and were staring into the swirling murky waters, their expressions frozen in openmouthed horror.

"Larry! Larry!" I was screaming the name over and over without realizing it.

The canoe continued to slide rapidly down the churning waters.

Larry didn't come up.

"Larry!"

Behind me, Tommy and Chris also called out his name, their voices shrill and frightened.

Where was he? Why didn't he swim to the surface?

The canoe was drifting farther and farther downriver.

"Larrrrrry!"

"We have to stop!" I screamed. "We have to slow down!"

"We can't!" Chris shouted back. "We don't know how!"

Still no sign of Larry. I realized he must be in trouble.

Without thinking, I tossed my paddle into the river, climbed to my feet, and plunged into the murky swirling waters to save him.

I jumped without thinking and swallowed a mouthful of water as I went down.

My heart thudded in my chest as I struggled frantically to the surface, sputtering and choking.

Gasping in a deep breath, I lowered my head and tried to swim against the current. My sneakers felt as if they weighed a thousand pounds.

I realized I should have pulled them off before I jumped.

The water heaved and tossed. I moved my arms in long, desperate strokes, pulling myself toward the spot where Larry had fallen. Glancing back, I saw the canoe, a dark blur growing smaller and smaller.

"Wait!" I wanted to shout to Tommy and Chris. "Wait for me to get Larry!"

But I knew that they didn't know how to slow the canoe. They were helpless as the current carried them away.

Where was Larry?

I sucked in another mouthful of air — and froze as I felt a sharp cramp in my right leg.

The pain shot up through my entire right side.

I slid under the water and waited for the pain to lessen.

The cramp seemed to tighten until I could barely move my leg. Water rushed over me. I struggled to pull myself up to the surface.

As I choked in more air, I stroked rapidly and hard, pulling myself up, ignoring the sharp pain in my leg.

Hey!

What was that object floating just ahead of me? A piece of driftwood being carried by the current?

Murky water washed over me, blinding me, tossing me back. Sputtering, I pulled myself back up.

Water rolled down my face. I struggled to see. Larry!

He came floating right to me.

"Larry! Larry!" I managed to scream.

But he didn't answer me. I could see clearly now that he was floating facedown.

The leg cramp started to loosen up as I reached out with both arms and grabbed Larry's shoulders. I pulled his head up from the water, rolled him onto his back, and wrapped my arm around his neck. I was using the lifesaving technique my parents had taught me.

Turning downriver, I searched for the canoe. But the current had carried it out of sight.

I swallowed another mouthful of icy water. Choking, I held on to Larry. I kicked hard. My right leg still felt tight and weak, but at least the pain had gone. Kicking and pulling with my free hand, I dragged Larry toward the shore.

To my relief, the current helped. It seemed to pull in the same direction.

A few seconds later, I was close enough to shore to stand. Wearily, panting like a wild animal, I tottered to my feet and dragged Larry onto the wet mud of the shore.

Was he dead? Had he drowned before I reached him?

I stretched him out on his back and, still panting loudly, struggling to catch my breath, to stop my entire body from trembling, I leaned over him.

And he opened his eyes.

He stared up at me blankly, as if he didn't recognize me.

Finally, he whispered my name. "Billy," he choked out, "are we okay?"

Larry and I rested for a bit. Then we walked back to camp, following the river upstream.

We were soaked clear through and drenched with mud, but I didn't care. We were alive. We were okay. I had saved Larry's life.

We didn't talk much on the way back. It was taking every ounce of strength we had just to walk.

I asked Larry if he thought Tommy and Chris would be okay.

"Hope so," he muttered, breathing hard. "They'll probably ride to shore and walk back like us."

I took this opportunity to ask him again about Jay and Colin. I thought maybe Larry would tell me the truth since we were completely alone and since I had just saved his life.

But he insisted he didn't know anything about my two bunk mates. As we walked, he raised one hand and swore he didn't know anything at all.

"So many frightening things have happened," I muttered.

He nodded, keeping his eyes straight ahead. "It's been strange," he agreed.

I waited for him to say more. But he walked on in silence.

It took three hours to walk back. We hadn't traveled downriver as far as I had thought, but the muddy shore kept twisting and turning, making our journey longer.

As the camp came into view, my knees buckled and my legs nearly collapsed under me.

Breathing hard, drenched in perspiration, our clothes still damp and covered in mud, we trudged wearily onto the waterfront.

"Hey!" a voice called from the swim area. Uncle Al, dressed in baggy green sweats, came hurrying across the dirt to us. "What happened?" he asked Larry.

"We had an accident!" I cried, before Larry had a chance to reply.

"I fell in," Larry admitted, his face reddening beneath the splattered mud. "Billy jumped in and saved me. We walked back."

"But Tommy and Chris couldn't stop the canoe. They drifted away!" I cried.

"We both nearly drowned," Larry told the frowning camp director. "But Billy — he saved my life."

"Can you send someone to find Tommy and Chris?" I asked, suddenly starting to shake all over, from exhaustion, I guess.

"The two boys floated on downriver?" Uncle Al asked, staring hard at Larry, scratching the back of his fringe of yellow hair.

Larry nodded.

"We have to find them!" I insisted, trembling harder.

Uncle Al continued to glare at Larry. "What about my canoe?" he demanded angrily. "That's our best canoe! How am I supposed to replace it?"

Larry shrugged unhappily.

"We'll have to go look for that canoe tomorrow," Uncle Al snapped.

He doesn't care about the two boys, I realized. *He doesn't care about them at all.*

"Go get into dry clothes," Uncle Al instructed Larry and me. He stormed off toward the lodge, shaking his head.

I turned and started for the cabin, feeling chilled, my entire body still trembling. I could feel a strong wave of anger sweep over me.

I had just saved Larry's life, but Uncle Al didn't care about that.

And he didn't care that two campers were lost on the river.

He didn't care that two campers and a counselor never returned from their hike.

He didn't care that boys were attacked by *creatures*!

He didn't care that kids disappeared and were never mentioned again.

He didn't care about any of us.

He only cared about his canoe.

My anger quickly turned to fear.

Of course, I had no way of knowing that the *scariest* part of my summer was still to come.

I was all alone in the bunk that night.

I pulled an extra blanket onto my bed and slid into a tight ball beneath the covers. I wondered if I'd be able to fall asleep. Or if my frightened, angry thoughts would keep me tossing and turning for another night.

But I was so weary and exhausted, even the eerie, mournful howls from the Forbidden Bunk couldn't keep me awake.

I fell into deep blackness and didn't wake up until I felt someone shaking my shoulders.

Startled alert, I sat straight up. "Larry!" I cried, my voice still clogged with sleep. "What's happening?"

I squinted across the room. Larry's bed was rumpled, the blanket balled up at the end. He had obviously come in late and slept in the bunk.

But Tommy's and Chris's beds were still untouched from the day before.

"Special hike," Larry said, walking over to his bunk. "Hurry. Get dressed."

"Huh?" I stretched and yawned. Outside the window, it was still gray. The sun hadn't risen. "What kind of hike?"

"Uncle Al called a special hike," Larry replied, his back to me. He grabbed the sheet and started to make his bed.

With a groan, I lowered myself to the cabin floor. It felt cold beneath my bare feet. "Don't we get to rest? I mean, after what happened yesterday?" I glanced once again at Tommy's and Chris's unused beds.

"It's not just us," Larry replied, smoothing the sheet. "It's the whole camp. Everyone's going. Uncle Al is leading it."

I pulled on a pair of jeans, stumbling across the cabin with one leg in. A sudden feeling of dread fell over me. "It wasn't scheduled," I said darkly. "Where is Uncle Al taking us?"

Larry didn't reply.

"Where?" I repeated shrilly.

He pretended he didn't hear me.

"Tommy and Chris — they didn't come back?" I asked glumly, pulling on my sneakers. Luckily, I had brought two pairs. My shoes from yesterday sat in the corner, still soaked through and mud-covered.

"They'll turn up," Larry replied finally. But he didn't sound as if he meant it.

120

I finished getting dressed, then ran up the hill to get breakfast. It was a warm, gray morning. It must have rained during the night. The tall grass glistened wetly.

Yawning and blinking against the harsh gray light, campers headed quietly up the hill. I saw that most of them had the same confused expression I had.

Why were we going on this unscheduled hike so early in the morning? How long was it going to be? Where were we going?

I hoped that Uncle Al or one of the counselors would explain everything to us at breakfast, but none of them appeared in the mess hall.

We ate quietly, without the usual joking around.

I found myself thinking about the terrifying canoe trip yesterday. I could almost taste the brackish water again. I saw Larry coming toward me, facedown, floating on the churning water like a clump of seaweed.

I pictured myself trying to get to him, struggling to swim, struggling to go against the current, to keep afloat in the swirls of white water.

And I saw a blur of the canoe as the strong river current carried it out of sight.

Suddenly, Dawn and Dori burst into my thoughts. I wondered if they were okay. I wondered if they were going to try to meet me again by the waterfront.

Breakfast was French toast with syrup. It was usually my favorite. But this morning, I just poked at it with my fork.

"Line up outside!" a counselor cried from the doorway.

Chairs scraped loudly. We all obediently climbed to our feet and began making our way outside.

Where are they taking us?

Why doesn't anyone tell us what this is about?

The sky had brightened to pink, but the sun still hadn't risen over the horizon.

We formed a single line along the side wall of the lodge. I was near the end of the line toward the bottom of the hill.

Some kids were cracking jokes and playfully shoving each other. But most were standing quietly or leaning against the wall, waiting to see what was going to happen.

Once the line was formed, one of the counselors walked the length of it, pointing his finger and moving his lips in concentration as he counted us. He counted us twice to make sure he had the right number.

Then Uncle Al appeared at the front of the line. He wore a brown-and-green camouflage outfit, the kind soldiers wear. He had on very black sunglasses, even though the sun wasn't up yet.

He didn't say a word. He signaled to Larry and another counselor, who were both carrying very large, heavy-looking brown bags over their shoulders. Then Uncle Al strode quickly down the hill, his eyes hidden behind the dark glasses, his features set in a tight frown.

He stopped in front of the last camper. "This way!" he announced loudly, pointing toward the waterfront.

Those were his only words. "This way!"

And we began to follow, walking at a pretty fast clip. Our sneakers slid against the wet grass. A few kids were giggling about something behind me.

To my surprise, I realized I was now nearly at the front of the line. I was close enough to call out to Uncle Al. So I did. "Where are we going?" I shouted.

He quickened his pace and didn't reply.

"Uncle Al — is this a long hike?" I called.

He pretended he hadn't heard.

I decided to give up.

He led us toward the waterfront, then turned right. Thick clumps of trees stood a short way up ahead where the river narrowed.

Glancing back to the end of the line, I saw Larry and the other counselor, bags on their shoulders, hurrying to catch up to Uncle Al.

What is this about? I wondered.

And as I stared at the clumps of low, tangled trees up ahead, a thought pushed its way into my head.

I can escape.

The thought was so frightening — but suddenly so real — it took a long time to form.

I can escape into these trees.

I can run away from Uncle Al and this frightening camp.

The idea was so exciting, I nearly stumbled over my own feet. I bumped into the kid ahead of me, a big bruiser of a guy named Tyler, and he turned and glared at me.

Whoa, I told myself, feeling my heart start to pound in my chest. *Think about this. Think carefully. . . .*

I kept my eyes locked on the woods. As we drew closer, I could see that the thick trees, so close together that their branches were all intertwined, seemed to stretch on forever.

They'd never find me in there, I told myself. *It would be really easy to hide in those woods.*

But then what?

I couldn't stay in the woods forever.

Then what?

Staring at the trees, I forced myself to concentrate, forced myself to think clearly.

I could follow the river. Yes. Stay on the shore.

Follow the river. It was bound to come to a town eventually. It *had* to come to a town.

I'd walk to the first town. Then I'd call my parents.

I can do it, I thought, so excited I could barely stay in line.

I just have to run. Make a dash for it. When no one is looking. Into the woods. Deep into the woods.

We were at the edge of the trees now. The sun had pulled itself up, brightening the rose-colored morning sky. We stood in the shadows of the trees.

I can do it, I told myself.

Soon.

My heart thudded loudly. I was sweating even though the air was still cool.

Calm down, Billy, I warned myself. *Just calm down.*

Wait your chance.

Wait till the time is right.

Then leave Camp Nightmare behind. Forever.

Standing in the shade, I studied the trees. I spotted a narrow path into the woods a few yards up head.

I tried to calculate how long it would take me to reach the path. Probably ten seconds at most. And then in another five seconds, I could be into the protection of the trees.

I can do it, I thought.

I can be gone in less than ten seconds.

I took a deep breath. I braced myself. I tensed my leg muscles, preparing to run.

Then I glanced to the front of the line.

To my horror, Uncle Al was staring directly at me. And he held a rifle in his hands.

I cried out when I saw the rifle in his hands.

Had he read my thoughts? Did he know I was about to make a run for it?

A cold chill slid down my back as I gaped at the rifle. As I raised my eyes to Uncle Al's face, I realized he wasn't looking at me.

He had turned his attention to the two counselors. They had lowered the bags to the ground and were bending over them, trying to get them open.

"Why did we stop?" Tyler, the kid ahead of me, asked.

"Is the hike over?" another kid joked. A few kids laughed.

"Guess we can go back now," another kid said.

I stood watching in disbelief as Larry and the other counselor began unloading rifles from the two bags.

"Line up and get one," Uncle Al instructed us,

tapping the handle of his own rifle against the ground. "One rifle per boy. Come on — hurry!"

No one moved. I think everyone thought Uncle Al was kidding or something.

"What's *wrong* with you boys? I said *hurry!*" he snapped angrily. He grabbed up an armload of rifles and began moving down the line, pushing one into each boy's hands.

He pushed a rifle against my chest so hard, I staggered back a few steps. I grabbed it by the barrel before it fell to the ground.

"What's going on?" Tyler asked me.

I shrugged, studying the rifle with horror. I'd never held any kind of real gun before. My parents were both opposed to firearms of all kinds.

A few minutes later, we were all lined up in the shadow of the trees, each holding a rifle. Uncle Al stood near the middle of the line and motioned us into a tight circle so we could hear him.

"What's going on? Is this target practice?" one boy asked.

Larry and the other counselor snickered at that. Uncle Al's features remained hard and serious.

"Listen up," he barked. "No more jokes. This is serious business."

The circle of campers tightened around him. We grew silent. A bird squawked noisily in a nearby tree. Somehow it reminded me of my plan to escape.

Was I about to be really sorry that I hadn't made a run for it?

"Two girls escaped from the girls' camp last night," Uncle Al announced in a flat, businesslike tone. "A blonde and a redhead."

Dawn and Dori! I exclaimed to myself. *I'll bet it was them!*

"I believe," Uncle Al continued, "that these are the same two girls who sneaked over to the boys' camp and hid near the waterfront a few days ago."

Yes! I thought happily. *It* is *Dawn and Dori! They escaped!*

I suddenly realized a broad smile had broken out on my face. I quickly forced it away before Uncle Al could see my happy reaction to the news.

"The two girls are in these woods, boys. They're nearby," Uncle Al continued. He raised his rifle. "Your guns are loaded. Aim carefully when you see them. They won't get away from us!"

"Huh?" I gasped in disbelief. "You mean we're supposed to *shoot* them?"

I glanced around the circle of campers. They all looked as dazed and confused as I did.

"Yeah. You're supposed to shoot them," Uncle Al replied coldly. "I *told* you — they're trying to escape."

"But we can't!" I cried.

"It's easy," Uncle Al said. He raised his rifle to his shoulder and pretended to fire it. "See? Nothing to it."

"But we can't kill people!" I insisted.

"Kill?" His expression changed behind the dark glasses. "I didn't say anything about killing, did I? These guns are loaded with tranquilizer darts. We just want to stop these girls — not hurt them."

Uncle Al took two steps toward me, the rifle still in his hands. He stood over me menacingly, lowering his face close to mine.

"You got a problem with that, Billy?" he demanded.

He was challenging me.

I saw the other boys back away.

The woods grew silent. Even the bird stopped squawking.

"You got a problem with that?" Uncle Al repeated, his face so close to mine, I could smell his sour breath.

Terrified, I took a step back, then another.

Why was he doing this to me? Why was he challenging me like this?

I took a deep breath and held it. Then I screamed as loudly as I could: "I — I won't do it!"

Without completely realizing what I was doing, I raised the rifle to my shoulder and aimed the barrel at Uncle Al's chest.

"You're gonna be sorry," Uncle Al growled in a low voice. He tore off the sunglasses and heaved them into the woods. Then he narrowed his eyes furiously at me. "Drop the rifle, Billy. I'm gonna make you sorry."

"No," I told him, standing my ground. "You're not. Camp is over. You're not going to do anything."

My legs were trembling so hard, I could barely stand.

But I wasn't going to go hunting Dawn and Dori. I wasn't going to do anything else Uncle Al said. Ever.

131

"Give me the rifle, Billy," he said in his low, menacing voice. He reached out a hand toward my gun. "Hand it over, boy."

"No!" I cried.

"Hand it over now," he ordered, his eyes narrowed, burning into mine. "Now!"

"No!" I cried.

He blinked once. Twice.

Then he leaped at me.

I took a step back with the rifle aimed at Uncle Al — and pulled the trigger.

The rifle emitted a soft *pop*.

Uncle Al tossed his head back and laughed. He let his rifle drop to the ground at his feet.

"Hey!" I cried out, confused. I kept the rifle aimed at his chest.

"Congratulations, Billy," Uncle Al said, grinning warmly at me. "You passed." He stepped forward and reached out his hand to shake mine.

The other campers dropped their rifles. Glancing at them, I saw that they were all grinning, too. Larry, also grinning, flashed me a thumbs-up sign.

"What's going on?" I demanded suspiciously. I slowly lowered the rifle.

Uncle Al grabbed my hand and squeezed it hard. "Congratulations, Billy. I *knew* you'd pass."

"Huh? I don't understand!" I screamed, totally frustrated.

But instead of explaining anything to me, Uncle Al turned to the trees and shouted, "Okay, everyone! It's over! He passed! Come out and congratulate him!"

And as I stared in disbelief, my wide-open mouth hanging down around my knees, people began stepping out from behind the trees.

First came Dawn and Dori.

"You *were* hiding in the woods!" I cried.

They laughed in response. "Congratulations!" Dawn cried.

And then others came out, grinning and congratulating me. I screamed when I recognized Mike. He was okay!

Beside him were Jay and Roger!

Colin stepped out of the woods, followed by Tommy and Chris. All smiling and happy and okay.

"What — what's going *on* here?" I stammered. I was totally stunned. I felt dizzy.

I didn't get it. I really didn't get it.

And then my mom and dad stepped out from the trees. Mom rushed up and gave me a hug. Dad patted the top of my head. "I knew you'd pass, Billy," he said. I could see happy tears in his eyes.

Finally, I couldn't take it anymore. I pushed Mom gently away. "Passed *what*?" I demanded. "What *is* this? What's going on?"

Uncle Al put his arm around my shoulders and guided me away from the group of campers. Mom and Dad followed close behind.

"This isn't really a summer camp," Uncle Al explained, still grinning at me, his face bright pink. "It's a government testing lab."

"Huh?" I swallowed hard.

"You know your parents are scientists, Billy," Uncle Al continued. "Well, they're about to leave on a very important expedition. And this time they wanted to take you along with them."

"How come you didn't tell me?" I asked my parents.

"We couldn't!" Mom exclaimed.

"According to government rules, Billy," Uncle Al continued, "children aren't allowed to go on official expeditions unless they pass certain tests. That's what you've been doing here. You've been taking tests."

"Tests to see what?" I demanded, still dazed.

"Well, we wanted to see if you could obey orders," Uncle Al explained. "You passed when you refused to go to the Forbidden Bunk." He held up two fingers. "Second, we had to test your bravery. You demonstrated that by rescuing Larry." He held up a third finger. "Third, we had to see if you knew when *not* to follow orders. You passed that test by refusing to hunt for Dawn and Dori."

"And everyone was in on it?" I asked. "All the campers? The counselors? Everyone? They were all actors?"

Uncle Al nodded. "They all work here at the

testing lab." His expression turned serious. "You see, Billy, your parents want to take you to a very dangerous place, perhaps the most dangerous place in the known universe. So we had to make sure you can handle it."

The most dangerous place in the universe?

"Where?" I asked my parents. "Where are you taking me?"

"It's a very strange planet called Earth," Dad replied, glancing at Mom. "It's very far from here. But it could be exciting. The inhabitants there are weird and unpredictable, and no one has ever studied them."

Laughing, I stepped between my mom and dad and put my arms around them. "Earth?! It sounds pretty weird. But it could *never* be as dangerous or exciting as Camp Nightmoon!" I exclaimed.

"We'll see," Mom replied quietly. "We'll see."

BEHIND THE SCREAMS

WELCOME TO CAMP NIGHTMARE

CONTENTS

Bonus material written and compiled
by Matthew D. Payne

About the Author

R.L. Stine's books are read all over the world. So far, his books have sold more than 300 million copies, making him one of the most popular children's authors in history. Besides Goosebumps, R.L. Stine has written the teen series Fear Street, the funny series Rotten School, as well as the Mostly Ghostly series, The Nightmare Room series, and the two-book thriller *Dangerous Girls*. R.L. Stine lives in New York with his wife, Jane, and Minnie, his King Charles spaniel. You can learn more about him at www.RLStine.com.

Q & A with R.L. Stine

Readers are certainly surprised by the twist ending of *Welcome to Camp Nightmare*. How did you ever think of it?

R.L. Stine (RLS): *I have a twisted mind. In fact, I have to go to a special doctor every month to have it UN-twisted. Not really—but I spend a lot of time trying to come up with crazy endings to surprise my readers. Did you know that I always think of the surprise ending first?*

The kids and counselors at Camp Nightmoon were very good at keeping secrets. How good are you at keeping a secret?

RLS: *I'll never tell!*

If you were sent to Camp Nightmoon, would you be able to pass Uncle Al's three tests?

RLS: *No way. I was a terrible camper. I hated the outdoors. I always wanted to be indoors, writing stories. I was so terrified of the swimming test at camp, I hid in the woods from the swimming counselor! To this day, I think about how scared I was when I had to jump into the pool. It helps me write scenes where kids are really scared.*

Can you swim? Have you ever experienced rapids like the ones that almost killed Larry in Chapter 17?

RLS: *We don't get too many rapids here in New York City, so I think I'm safe! But you know what? It's raining right now, so I'd better be careful. Some of the puddles are pretty deep!*

If you HAD to choose one, which would you rather be bitten by—a bear or a snake?

RLS: *Too late. I was already bitten—by a vampire!*

What was the scariest book you read as a kid? And which Goosebumps do you think is really scary?

RLS: *The scariest book I read as a kid was a Ray Bradbury novel called* Something Wicked This Way Comes. *It's about two boys in the Midwest who sneak out of their houses late at night and go to a mysterious—and very evil—carnival. A terrifying book! It creeped me out—and it also had a big influence on me and my writing.*

I think Goosebumps HorrorLand #12: The Streets of Panic Park *might be one of the scariest books I ever wrote. The villain at Panic Park—he's called The Menace—is a really scary dude. He's so out of control, you don't know how far he'll go to terrify everyone!*

Goosebumps HorrorLand #15: *Heads, You Lose!* has a running theme of "making your own luck." Do you believe in luck, and how does it affect the adventures of your characters?

RLS: *Do I believe in luck? I don't know. Let's flip a coin! Seriously, horrible things happen to all the kids in Goosebumps books. I think it's very bad luck to turn into a monster or be haunted by a howling ghost or be chased down the street by a living dummy! In my books, you've got to be lucky to survive!*

To find out R.L. Stine's advice when it comes to dealing with ghosts, pick up the special collector's edition of *GHOST BEACH*.

Top Ten Reasons to
Be Happy Your Camp Is Haunted

The lake of fire is really hard to swim in, and a few of your friends have been carried off by that pesky pack of vampire bats. But there are plenty of benefits to spending the summer at a haunted camp. Here are just a few. . . .

10 The talking Brussels sprouts make food fights much more interesting.

9 The tents all float a few inches off the ground, giving campers a much more comfortable sleep.

8 Since the camp counselors only come out at night, you're free to do whatever you want during the day.

7 Pick up the right baseball bat, and you're guaranteed to hit a home run every time you step up to the plate. (This really makes up for the fact that if you pick up the wrong bat, you'll lose all of your fingers.)

6 All the ghosts packed into your cabin make it nice and cool even during the hottest summer nights.

5 The werewolves' howls keep all the bears away.

4 You can brush up on your history by talking with some of the really old ghosts floating around.

3 The haunted bands that play in the abandoned theater are AMAZING!

2 The giant spiders eat all the mosquitoes, gnats, and other annoying things like stupid bunk mates.

1 The meat at the cafeteria is never tough—it's always fresh and young.

Venomous Snake Stats

Not all snakes are **VENOMOUS**. In fact, most are not. Only 1 in 4 of the earth's snakes use venom for hunting or self-defense.

There is no easy way to tell a venomous snake from a nonvenomous one. A bite from any snake can cause damage and infection. It's best to treat any snake bite as if it were poisonous. Seek medical attention immediately, just like Mike did in Chapter 5. Hopefully, you'll have a better time finding a nurse.

Of all the venomous snakes, there are a few that really stand out. The **BLACK MAMBA** is one of the most dangerous snakes and also one of the fastest. It can slither more than 12 miles per hour—faster than most kids, unless they are riding a bike! This combination of venom and speed (along with a really bad attitude) makes the black mamba one of the world's deadliest snakes.

The Rinkhals, or spitting cobra, can spit venom more than 8 feet. It will aim for the face of its prey. If the venom gets in the eyes, it can cause great pain or even **BLINDNESS**. The Rinkhals has been known to play dead, lying on the ground with its mouth open. This can trick an approaching animal long enough for the Rinkhals to strike.

The award for deadliest venom goes to the inland taipan of Australia, which has the most potent venom of any snake in the world. In fact, Australia boasts 5 of the top 10 most venomous snakes in the world.

Despite being a land of venomous snakes, Australia has a very small number of snake bite deaths—under 10 per year. The United States has a similarly low amount as well. India and Sri Lanka have the largest number of occurrences of snake bite deaths every year.

We end with true snake royalty—the king cobra. Why are we mentioning **HIS ROYAL HIGHNESS**? Because the king cobra is the longest venomous snake in the world. It can measure up to 22 feet. Its venom is less potent than other snakes, but because of its size and ability to inject large doses of venom, it is one of the world's deadliest snakes.

DICTIONARY TIME!

Snakes are "venomous," not "poisonous." Poison is breathed, eaten, or absorbed through the skin. Venom is injected. Now go impress your science teacher with that bit of knowledge!

CREATE A CREEPY CAMP SCHEDULE!

If you were a ghoulish camp counselor, what ghastly activities would you put together for your campers? Check out below our example of a really creepy day at camp and then make your own schedule. Have a friend make one, too. Whose schedule is scarier?

Tips for creating a schedule to scream for are found after our example.

** SCHEDULE FOR CAMP BLOODSTONE**

7:45 A.M. Screaming Banshees Wake Up All Campers

8:00 Breakfast—Frosted Flakes of Skin with Bat Milk

9:00 Cabin Inspection (Monsters under beds and skeletons in closets are fed.)

9:30 - 10:45 Dirt Nap

10:45 – 12:00 Tennis with Shrunken Heads

12:00 - 1:00 P.M. Lunch—Freshly ground yak burgers—hair and horn included!

1:00 - 2:15 Personal Time (Write a letter or make a call to your parents . . . if they haven't cut the phone lines yet. . . .)

2:15 – 4:00 Swimming with Alligators

4:00 – 5:30 Zombie Archery

5:30 Dinner—SPECIAL TONIGHT: We're putting on a murder mystery, and one of our campers will have the starring role!

7:30 – 9:30 A preview of tonight's horrors: haunted tales around the campfire.

10:00 LIGHTS-OUT! No, really. We mean it. . . .

TIPS!

CHOW TIME: Make sure to think of gruesome things to eat for breakfast, lunch, and dinner. Feel free to throw in a snack or two, as well. Think of what a monster would eat—vampires and blood or zombies and brains. Or think of the most disgusting thing you'd never want to eat. Like a slug. But make it part of a normal meal. Like a slug sandwich. Or spaghetti with slug sauce.

ACTIVITIES: Think of all the activities you would normally do at a camp and then add a silly, scary twist. For instance, we took tennis and added the element of shrunken heads. You can also add dangerous activities that would never be found at a camp like Swimming with Alligators or Hang Gliding with Vultures.

PUT YOURSELF IN A CAMPER'S SHOES: What else happens during a day at camp? Sing-alongs, cabin inspections, talent contests, campouts, mail call . . .

REMEMBER: Be scary AND funny!

DOUBLE THE FRIGHT
ALL AT ONE SITE
www.scholastic.com/goosebumps

FIENDS OF GOOSEBUMPS & GOOSEBUMPS HORRORLAND CAN:

- **PLAY GHOULISH GAMES!**

- **CHAT WITH FELLOW FAN-ATICS!**

- **WATCH CLIPS FROM SPINE-TINGLING DVDs!**

- **EXPLORE CLASSIC BOOKS AND NEW TERROR-IFIC TITLES!**

- **CHECK OUT THE GOOSEBUMPS HORRORLAND VIDEO GAME!**

- **GET GOOSEBUMPS PHOTOSHOCK FOR THE IPHONE™ OR IPOD TOUCH®!**

SCHOLASTIC

GBWEB

The Original Bone-Chilling Series

—with Exclusive
Author Interviews!

NIGHT of the LIVING DUMMY
R.L. STINE

DEEP TROUBLE
R.L. STINE

MONSTER BLOOD
R.L. STINE

The HAUNTED MASK
R.L. STINE

ONE DAY at HORRORLAND
R.L. STINE

The CURSE of the MUMMY'S TOMB
R.L. STINE

BE CAREFUL WHAT YOU WISH FOR
R.L. STINE

SAY CHEESE and DIE!
R.L. STINE

The HORROR at CAMP JELLYJAM
R.L. STINE

HOW I GOT MY SHRUNKEN HEAD
R.L. STINE

R. L. Stine's Fright Fest!
Now with Splat Stats and More!

THERE'S ALWAYS ROOM FOR ONE MORE SCREAM!

An all-new series from fright-master R.L. Stine!

CLAWS!
R.L. STINE

NIGHT OF THE GIANT EVERYTHING
R.L. STINE

THE FIVE MASKS OF DR. SCREEM
R.L. STINE

WHY I QUIT ZOMBIE SCHOOL
R.L. STINE

DON'T SCREAM!
R.L. STINE

THE BIRTHDAY PARTY OF NO RETURN!
R.L. STINE

Catch the MOST WANTED Goosebumps® villains UNDEAD OR ALIVE!

■ SCHOLASTIC

scholastic.com/goosebumps

Available in print and eBook editions

GBMW9

NOW A MAJOR
MOTION PICTURE

JACK BLACK

Goosebumps